A TASTE FOR MURDER

"I have a suspicion that Hurley is more involved in Mary Lou's death than he's let on."

"What do you think, that he murdered her?" Sam said with a chuckle.

"Yes, I do."

Sam's eyes widened with surprise. "Hurley Booker killed his wife? You conclude that from the conversation you've had today?"

"Not just today but ever since her death. You know I've always thought that death by her own hand made no sense. Now that I've found out about Mary Lou's possible affair, Hurley's infidelity, and the details of Mary Lou's marriage—the pieces are coming together."

"What pieces?" Sam's concern for Bailey showed in his voice. "Hurley is a respected doctor. Yolanda is a grieving mother. An unaffectionate man whose wife is cheating on him isn't necessarily a suspect for murder."

"In this case, to me, he is."

DELICIOUS
SHELBY LEWIS

PINNACLE BOOKS
KENSINGTON PUBLISHING CORP.

PINNACLE BOOKS are published by

Kensington Publishing Corp.
850 Third Avenue
New York, NY 10022

Pinnacle and the P logo Reg. U.S. Pat. & TM Off.

First Printing: January, 1996

Printed in the United States of America

Dedicated to Kimberly Antonia

"Intuition is like reading a word without having to spell it out. A child can't do that because it has had so little experience. But a grown-up person knows the word because they've seen it often before. You catch my meaning, Vicar?"

"Yes," I said slowly. "I think I do. You mean that if a thing reminds you of something else—well, it's probably the same kind of thing."

"Exactly."

—from *Murder at the Vicarage* by Agatha Christie

Prologue

He stood completely still, staring at her quietly. The knuckle bones of his hands showed in stark relief against his flesh. He knew what he had to do, but he chose to gaze upon her face and body one more time. Standing on the deck of the boat, he studied her priceless features. He had always thought she was beautiful, but she never looked as beautiful to him in the past as she did at that moment. He sighed wistfully. He should have made love with her first. But, there was no time for that now.

His eyes traversed upward, beginning at her feet, ending with the top of her head. The teal silk pants she wore were soft and full in the legs, tapered at the ankle. The cream blouse she'd tucked into the waistband of her pants was made of sandwashed silk, its front and back formed a u-neckline that showed off her splendid collarbones. One of her long, brown arms was flung across her forehead to block the sun from her eyes. He liked every inch of her flawless body. But what she had done, well, he couldn't ignore.

He walked up to her, his mission clear. If they couldn't make love, he at least wanted a kiss goodbye. It wasn't that he would easily forget her—not the scent of her perfume, or the feel of her hair—he wanted to feel once more those damnable lips, the ones that had ruined his life in the space of a heartbeat telling him things that were best kept secret. But that was in the past.

Gently, he went to her. The alarm in her eyes showed she questioned his motives. Hadn't they said horrible things to each other less than an hour before? What a shame, he thought after the kiss. Her ripe, red-painted mouth fell open in horror as he pushed his palms hard against her chest. He smiled at her reaction. Nothing else mattered now, except one thing. Leaning over the ship's edge, he finished the scream she had only just begun.

A Fish Fry for Fifty People

Fried Catfish
Okra Spread
Black-eyed Pea Salad
Hush Puppies
Green Beans with Ham Hocks
Sweet Potato Pie
Lemonade with Mint Sprigs
Coffee and Tea

One

It was Sunday. A mid-afternoon breeze ruffled the soft, supple leaves of the gnarled old oak trees in the front and side yards of 1899 Laurel Lane in New Hope, California, home to thirty-year-old Bailey Walker, her husband, Sam, and their daughter, Fern. A part-time caterer, Bailey hustled about her kitchen to prepare enough for a private gathering of fifty family and friends. She planned to serve it on Monday at a funeral reception in honor of one of her best friends, Mary Lou Booker, a freelance muralist and loving mother.

The suicide confirmation had permitted Mary Lou's husband, Hurley, to proceed with funeral and burial arrangements at Maple Lawn, one of New Hope's finest cemeteries, an impressive expanse of green lawn, towering maple trees, and rambling yellow roses. Maple Lawn dated to the 1800s when the mostly black township of 150,000 people had its beginnings. Bailey considered the location beautiful, like the woman who would rest there in final peace.

Bailey had easily accepted Hurley's request that she cater his wife's funeral reception. For her the preparation of the meal was a tribute to the treasured friendship she had once shared with Mary Lou. During her

friend's life, the two women had met most Friday
mornings for coffee and pastries. They would take
turns hosting the informal meeting in each other's
kitchens, their favorite places to chat after taking their
eight-year-old daughters to school. On their last Friday
together, it had been Mary Lou's turn to host.

Dressed in a slim pair of blue jeans and a sapphire-
colored cotton shirt, Bailey pulled a red plastic tub
from her pantry, ready to prepare the large meal. Rins-
ing the tub at the double sink, she swished it dry with
a thick dish towel then gathered the ingredients she
needed to prepare the fresh catfish she and Hurley
planned as the main entree: flour, cornmeal, eggs, oil,
and seasonings. A bowl of fresh lemons sat in a stainless steel colander, awaiting their turn with her deft
ministrations for use as garnish on the fish platters the
next day.

When the purr of the telephone caught her attention,
Bailey dusted her hands across the hunter-green apron
she wore around her waist. Intercepting the third ring,
she said, "Hello, who's calling please?"

"It's me. Ardene. I got all the catfish you wanted."

Bailey recognized the raspy smoker's voice on the
other end of the line immediately. Ardene Donaldson
was her contact in the seafood industry. Through Ardene, she purchased quality fish throughout the year
at reasonable prices.

"Excellent," Bailey complimented her, "and right
on time, as usual." In exchange for the courtesy of
front-door seafood deliveries, she catered a summer-
time birthday party for Ardene's twin daughters, Ra-
mona and Lisa, at a reduced rate.

"I'm just about ready to bring the fish by," Ardene

explained, glad to help Bailey pull off a rush catering assignment.

Bailey glanced at the gold wristwatch strapped to her left arm to confirm the time. "I'll be here. Just honk the van horn when you pull in the drive."

A brief pause on the telephone line let Bailey know Ardene was troubled. That knowledge was not due to her intuition—Ardene always paused before introducing a tense subject into conversation. "Ain't it kinda weird frying fish for a funeral reception?"

Because the menu was not a traditional one, Bailey was prepared for a bit of ribbing on the subject, the reason her answer was as prompt as it was simply spoken. "Mary Lou loved catfish. I loved Mary Lou."

"Heard that," Ardene demurred. She had met Mary Lou once, when dropping off a seafood order at Bailey's house and had considered Mary Lou a pleasant woman. "See ya in an hour."

The telephone business complete, Bailey moved on to prepare the okra spread. She needed firm garden okra, fresh garlic, onion, pepper, salt, Tabasco, and water. While the water came to a boil, she worked in systematic precision to remove the stems and tips off the rinsed okra, slicing each piece into fourths. Next she chopped the onion and garlic. Then to her irritation the telephone rang again. She lifted the receiver in the middle of the second ring. "Hello?"

"It's Minette," a warm and cultured voice responded. "What are you up to?" A hospital administrator, Minette Ramsey was Bailey's other best girlfriend. At five-feet-six-inches, Minette was a blackberry-toned woman with an hourglass figure who wore her relaxed hair in a chic short length.

"I'm making the food for Mary Lou's funeral reception," Bailey answered as she stopped to survey her efforts.

Minette's voice was laced with sorrow. "I phoned to say I'll help you serve the meal tomorrow. Will Sam and Fern be there, too?"

"Yes." Bailey's husband and daughter often helped at her jobs. Sam shared the lifting and carrying with Bailey. Fern made her parents proud by keeping an eye on the beverage table. She kept it tidy, poured liquids, and signaled her parents when the supplies needed restocking. Usually the sugar and creamer decanters were the first serving dishes to go low.

"Where are they now?" Minette asked, assuming Sam had taken Fern for an outing while Bailey spent time in the kitchen. Minette admired the way Sam supported Bailey by giving her quiet time when she needed it. Some days when she called, Minette discovered Sam had taken Fern off for father-daughter time while Bailey relaxed in the sun room or while she worked magic in her kitchen. Although Minette was a divorceé, she hoped to marry again one day and considered Sam Walker the kind of sound, loving man she wanted in her life.

Bailey smiled as she thought about him. "Sam's out running an errand. Fern's in the backyard starting seedlings in the greenhouse with her friend Jordanna." Sam had built the greenhouse for Bailey this year as a tenth-year-anniversary present. Just mentioning the greenhouse brought a lump to her throat. When Mary Lou had visited, the two women often sought the peace of the place Mary Lou always said put her in a meditative mood. The mood, she added, was enhanced by Bailey's hospitality and good food. These times were welcomed gifts by the women and they communed in good-natured sistership.

"Hey, did you hear my question?" Minette's voice pulled Bailey out of her reverie.

Bailey groaned. "Sorry. Ask me again."

"Has Fern ever attended a funeral event?" Fern was Minette's godchild. When she spent time with Fern, she often imagined having a child of her own. With the right man, she hoped she could.

"No, she hasn't. Sam and I don't want to short-change Fern's feelings for Mary Lou by glossing over death, hoping to protect her. We feel the truth is best, even when it hurts." Allowing Fern to attend Mary Lou's funeral had been a joint decision by Sam and Bailey, one the couple had discussed at length, deciding in the end not to shield her from death, a natural part of the life cycle.

Minette sighed. "I understand what you're saying, Bailey. I feel sorry for Hurley."

Bailey knew that in her role as hospital administrator, Minette worked with Hurley at Providence Hospital where he worked as a physician. Through Mary Lou, Bailey understood that Hurley headed several medical staff committees, a role that brought him into contact with Minette regularly.

"By keeping Fern with us, she can talk about her feelings to me and Sam as they come up. Last night she told me she didn't understand why I'm catering food when the occasion is a sad one."

"I've never heard of a catered funeral reception either. I admire your gumption."

Bailey explained why she was pleased to cater the

reception. "Cooking food in Mary Lou's honor helps me deal with her loss."

"I like the way Hurley is paying his last respects to Mary Lou in their home. She always said she loved her house." Minette spoke in a clear, reflective tone. She had run into Mary Lou at hospital social events and through the women's group she hosted in her own home every month. Knowing Mary Lou had been alive the previous Friday, then dead the next day made Minette shudder because it made her own mortality suddenly very real. More than ever she wanted what Bailey had: a loving and supportive husband and a healthy child of her own.

Confidence laced Bailey's voice. "I agree. Celebrating Mary Lou's life on her own turf is a good thing. I welcome your help tomorrow, Minette."

Minette understood the subtle hint from Bailey that she needed to get off the telephone in order to work. "No problem. I'll see you tomorrow."

Bailey hardly had a chance to hang up the telephone, when the kitchen nook door swung open to reveal her dungaree-clad daughter. Now that Fern's friend had gone home to clean up, Bailey's only child stood before her, spotted with mud. She and Jordanna had finished planting vegetable seeds, a task the girls enjoyed doing. Garden work allowed them the chance to get good and dirty without much complaint from their mothers.

Looking at Fern's ebony skin and equally dark hair, Bailey remembered an old southern superstition her grandmother taught her about children in the growing garden. According to the superstition, the fertile presence of children encouraged a garden to flourish.

Bailey was not sure if the superstition contained any merit, but her garden flourished every year.

"Look at you," she said with a smile as she took in her daughter's appearance and wrinkled her nose. Bits of packed mud clung to Fern's worn-out low-cut canvas sneakers. Her daughter swore she couldn't throw them away because they were so comfortable. It never bothered Fern that her sneakers had holes in the toes or that the laces were broken. As long as the sneakers stayed on the veranda, Bailey did not mind them, either.

"Leave your muddy socks outside with your sneakers, Fern. I'll get them later," she prompted, her tone firm and maternal. "Wash your hands and face too—with soap."

After Fern returned from the bathroom, Bailey crossed to the king-sized refrigerator and pulled a gallon jug of apple juice from the top shelf. "Oatmeal-raisin cookie?" she offered as a treat with the juice.

"No, thanks. Mom, when Jordanna gets back, is it okay if I ask her to spend the night?" Bailey remembered school was out the next day for a teacher's education session. The timing worked well for Sam and Bailey because Fern did not need to miss a day of school in order to attend the funeral and funeral reception. Sam had arranged a personal day off from work in order to attend.

"You know tomorrow is a special day. Let's invite Jordanna to spend the night with you on Friday." Bailey handed the cold cup of fruit juice to Fern. When she did, she noticed particles of rich soil still trapped beneath the child's fingernails. She and Jordanna refused to wear gloves in the garden. Without gloves,

Fern protested, they could sink their warm fingers into the cool, dark earth. Although she chastised her, Bailey did not blame the girls; she often did the same thing.

"Okay." Taking a seat at the countertop, Fern's eyes lit up as Bailey slid a bowl of seedless green grapes in her direction. Next to strawberries, green grapes were her favorite fruit. As Fern munched on grapes, she looked around her mother's kitchen. Whitewashed wood existed with white-enameled ceiling beams and a matching linoleum floor. Blue accents were placed in studied abandon throughout the many-windowed room. Because of all the windows, the kitchen was bathed in sunlight. She especially liked the African violets she had helped pot that grew and blossomed on the counter beside her.

Popping another grape in her mouth she ran the tip of one ebony finger along the decorative rims. On the far end of the counter by the telephone there was a potted pilea, its deep green leaves, streaked with silver, a fitting companion to its colorful cousins, the African violets.

"Would you and Jordanna like to play Suzy Mary?" Bailey suggested coyly to Fern knowing that Suzy Mary was the girls' favorite dress-up game. With Fern entertained until Sam returned, Bailey could work faster in the kitchen.

"Yes!" Fern shouted, excited at the prospect of spending more time with Jordanna, one of her closest friends.

"Good." Bailey smiled, her spirits lifted by Fern's enthusiasm. "After you call Jordanna, change into clean clothes. I'll be in the guest room, setting things up."

Fern beamed at her mother. "Can we have tea in the sun room, Mom?"

Bailey tugged one of Fern's heavy braids. "Of course you can."

"Thanks. I love you, Mom." Intense pleasure showed in Fern's brown eyes.

"And I love you," Bailey affirmed as Fern raced to her bedroom.

Bailey then washed her hands and dried them on the towel tossed over her left shoulder. Removing her apron, she headed to the guest room, located down a short hallway to the right of the den. The rose-colored guest room inspired romance in Bailey. Lush layers of rose-embroidered linen graced a solid oak bed. Atop the double bed were mounds of plump pillows shaped like hearts. Family photographs adorned a lace-draped dressing table. Twin bedside chests supported pink candlestick lamps. French lace embellished the vertical windows.

Pushed against the foot of the oak bed, was an aged cedar chest. Inside the chest were a half dozen vintage dresses, matching antique shoes, and a sparkling array of costume jewelry. The chest contents were all remnants of another woman's past, Bailey's maternal grandmother, Chloe. It had been Chloe who taught Bailey and her sister, Daphne, how to play Suzy Mary, a game they played during the long, hot days of summer.

Holding a string of multi-colored glass beads in her hands, Bailey studied her image in the mirror above the dressing table. She was a slender woman, five-feet-five-inches tall. Her deep ocher eyes were wide and clear. Matching narrow brows arced from the inner corner of her eyes to the outer corners in sleek perfection. She had a slightly pointed nose that was centered in pleasing proportion to her oblong face, its chin smooth and round. Full-sized lips parted to reveal even straight teeth. Red brown hair framed her cocoa colored face.

Glancing at a five-by-seven-inch color photograph of Sam on the dressing table, Bailey assessed her handsome husband. He was thirty-two-years-old and six feet tall. Like Fern, he was ebony hued. His hair grew in waves he combed away from a broad forehead. Jet-black eyes rested beneath a thick swathe of equally dark brows. His wide nose peaked above a strong upper lip, the first half of a particularly kissable set of sensual lips. Bailey agreed with her sister's opinion that Sam's warm, down-to-earth personality rivaled his sturdy physique.

"Where is everybody!" Jordanna hollered. Weighted down with dainty-faced dolls, play wigs, and pink feathered boas, Jordanna hammered on the Walkers' kitchen nook door, a mere formality, as she was already entering the house. Bailey always kept the door unlocked during the day which meant Fern could run in and out at will. It also meant Bailey would not be locked out of the house by mistake after dashing to the garden for an item she required in the kitchen.

"Hello, again, Miss Bailey," Jordanna greeted. While Fern was tall and skinny, Jordanna was short and plump. She wore flowered purple stretch pants with a matching top.

"We're back here!" Fern shouted from the guest room, her voice shrill as a whistle.

"Fern, stop shouting," Bailey admonished.

Fern's sincere apology could not dampen her excitement. She was armed with her best baby dolls, a tube of clear lipstick, face powder, and Tinker Bell perfume. Glowing, she anticipated the dress-up tea party for two.

Fern stopped digging in the costume jewelry box to glance at Bailey. "Oops! You forgot something, Mom."

Bailey looked around the guest room, recognizing it would be a complete disaster the next time she saw it. "No, I didn't," she said, smiling at Fern.

Jordanna burst into giggles, an action that exposed a jack-o-lantern set of teeth. Like Fern, she wore her hair in thick braids.

Fern smacked her lips, mildly annoyed with her mother's slow wit. "The hats, Mom. We can't play Suzy Mary without the hats!"

Bailey cast expressive eyes heavenward. "Of course," she remembered. "Silly me."

Enjoying Bailey's sense of humor, Jordanna giggled again.

Pulling an assortment of fancy hat boxes off the closet shelf, Bailey deposited the rose-scented bounty at her happy daughter's feet. "Have fun, girls. I'll have munchies ready in a few minutes."

"Thanks, Miss Bailey," Jordanna chimed, her eyes alight with pleasure. "You do a bunch of neat stuff."

"You're very welcome," Bailey replied, feeling good about passing on her childhood games to a new generation of children. Humming softly, she walked to the formal dining room, where she stored tea party ware. From the lemon-waxed buffet, Bailey pulled out a child's silver tea service, cutlery, inexpensive china, and an ivory lace table runner. Arms filled, she carefully made her way to the sun room where she arranged the party ware in fetching fashion on the wicker coffee table. In a crystal vase atop the table were black-eyed susans, tiny sunflowers, and purple dahlias.

On a two-tiered dessert tray she placed oatmeal-raisin cookies and assorted fruit. After filling the teapot with cinnamon herbal tea, she pushed a tape of songs into a cassette player. The tape was a gift to Fern from Minette. As the tape played "Little Sally Walker," Bailey pulled a pastel Victorian dollhouse from its distant corner in the sun room. With sunlight pouring through the glass ceiling onto the wicker love seat and chairs, she decided everything was perfect for the two giggling girls.

Alone once more in the kitchen, Bailey donned a fresh apron. Tossing a clean towel across her left shoulder, she concentrated on the black-eyed pea salad. On the tiled counter she placed cleaned peas, salt pork, onion, garlic cloves, celery, vinegar, sugar, vegetable oil, salt, and pepper. As she prepared to shake the salad vinegar, the insistent beep-beep of Ardene's van stopped her in stride. Flustered by how quickly the time had passed, Bailey grabbed an attractive tin of homemade lemon pound cake. Whenever Ardene delivered a special job on short notice, Bailey presented her with a small pastry. For this occasion she was grateful Ardene had brought the fish already cleaned and filleted, thus saving her valuable time in the kitchen.

As she opened the front door to greet her friend, Bailey wondered again why Mary Lou Booker, a devoted mother and fine mural artist, would plunge her body into the icy depths of the San Francisco Bay on the eve of her wedding anniversary.

A Bolstering Breakfast
for the Bereaved

Waffles
Pan-Fried Ham
Spicy Coffee
Cranapple Juice

Two

It was Monday. Morning dawned in beguiling, vivid splendor as Bailey raised the pale pink blinds at the windows of her pine furnished breakfast nook. With her family still asleep, she took a few seconds to admire the view. Rolling hills were distant vistas dotted with stands of live oak and narrow-leafed eucalyptus. The tranquil vision lightened Bailey's troubled mood by reminding her of the sheer, simple excellence in being alive. Easing her way out the kitchen door, she headed to the far right of her half acre lot to the fern garden, a setting Sam had designed to celebrate the birth of their daughter.

Breathing deeply, Bailey relished the richness of the dense shady garden. Wherever she turned there was a different shade of verdant green. She saw maidenhair ferns, ostrich ferns, cinnamon ferns, chain ferns, and lady ferns in abundance. The lush, healthy plants were all cast beneath the umbrella shaped foliage of wax myrtle trees, specimens beautifully accented with borders of sculpted boxwood, zephyr lilies, and Japanese anemone.

A tiny waterfall flattered the setting as it trickled slow and cool over round river rocks and smooth flat pebbles in pale shades of gray, yellow, and brown. It was a place where she could commune with nature while sitting on a time-worn bench made of weathered teak. The bench rested in an alcove created by a thriving set of what Fern called yesterday, today, and tomorrow trees, so named because of the fast changes the blossoms experienced throughout their season: from purple to lavender to white.

The small prized trees modeled the way Bailey felt about herself, a self which altered its shape to fit the fleeting events of a metered lifetime. On this solemn day she needed to absorb and to adapt to the reality of Mary Lou's suicide. Bailey viewed the warm May morning too lovely and good to prelude a solemn funeral event. On the other hand, the morning was appropriate because of her wonderful memories of Mary Lou. Those memories made her death so hard for Bailey to understand—and she was not sure if she ever could.

While Bailey finished cooking for the funeral reception on Sunday evening, Sam's muscles had rippled effortlessly as he packed the family's burgundy Previa. Inside the minivan had gone the various bits and pieces of Bailey's part-time business. The boxes Sam had packed away were filled with food supplies, serving items, backup sugar for the lemonade, extra condiments, napkins, forks, knives, and cups. Her family's commitment to her business endeavors added to Bailey's enjoyment of life in general.

Donning a bib apron to cover her dress, Bailey made breakfast for her family, beginning with the spicy coffee she always shared with Sam. She lifted a heavy metal saucepan from the cupboard into which she placed cold tap water, then boiled it. Next she added light brown sugar, whole allspice, orange peel, and dried cinnamon sticks. While this mixture boiled, she rolled a lemon across the countertop in order to release the juice inside. Once the lemon became soft to the touch, she sliced it in half, then squeezed out the liquid. She poured the lemon juice into the boiling mixture. Next she dropped and stirred coffee into the bubbling spices.

After cleaning up, Bailey set previously made waffle batter on top of the counter. She stirred the batter with a wooden spoon in order to loosen it. With a plastic ladle she plopped individual servings down onto a hot grid iron. While the waffles baked, she sliced strawberries for topping. The breakfast would be a hearty meal that would last her family until dinnertime.

The smell of hot bread, rich butter, and maple syrup had Fern rushing to finish making her bed. The salty scent of thick ham slices sizzling in a black iron skillet had Sam singing in the shower. The heady fragrance of spicy coffee in the making set Bailey's own stomach rumbling with anticipation, an expectation that brought a smile to her face.

Sam's heart quickened when he emerged from the bedroom, raring for breakfast, but he stopped cold at his first glimpse of Bailey in daylight. She was lovely, despite having been awake for hours, too keyed up to sleep. He knew about her disbelief and sadness over Mary Lou's death in addition to her unnecessary nervousness about the menu. "You're beautiful," he told her by way of greeting. Sam admired not only her beauty, mothering skills, and wifely tenderness, but her willpower, efficiency, and commitment to whatever she set out to do. He believed those qualities were the reasons her catering business was a steady success.

Sam was proud of Bailey. From their home, she began her business making food for neighborhood birthday parties and picnics. This venture led to catered dinner parties. By word of mouth her catering business blossomed like Bailey's garden. He recognized that the catering business helped her feel useful within the community. Sam bent his head to kiss his wife on her temple, a morning ritual. He loved the way her hair framed her face in a glowing sheen of hair scented like roses.

"You look gorgeous yourself," she complimented him, smiling back. Sam wore black pants with a matching leather belt and shoes. He topped the pants with a long-sleeved white shirt. Just as he stretched down toward his wife's lips for another special kiss, Fern skidded into the kitchen, ready for breakfast.

Fern was pretty in a prim black dress, its white collar an excellent contrast to the ebony cast of her skin. Watching her daughter move quickly to her favorite chair, Bailey grinned. She did not need a mirror to know, that with Fern by their side, she and Sam made a striking family.

After the funeral, Bailey applauded Hurley's choice of a traditional ceremony. Organized and purposeful, the public worship had provided a solid opportunity for family and friends to comfort one another. For Bailey, the reality of Mary Lou's death was still unsettling. Mary Lou had never seemed despondent or de-

pressed and her husband adored her. More than anything, Bailey wanted to understand how Mary Lou, so
devoted a mother, could do this to her daughter. It was
so out of character.

As they drove to Mary Lou's home to set up for the
funeral reception, Bailey swiveled in her seat in order
to face Fern. "It's not too late to stay with Jordanna.
Her mom said it's okay."

Bailey saw indecision on Fern's face before she
made up her mind. "No," she finally answered. "I
want to stay with you and Daddy."

"That's fine by us, sugar," Sam assured her, his deep
voice sincere. "We'd love your company." His fingers
wrapped loosely about the steering wheel, Sam veered
the minivan right on Lobelia Street to their destination
at 302 Daisy Lane.

In their neighborhood, most of the streets were
named after flowers, a lingering legacy from Melinda
Ray, foremother of New Hope and an avid gardener,
a woman whose comfortable old home now belonged
to the Walkers. Their old-fashioned farmhouse was as
homey as Mary Lou's house was modern. Symmetrical
in design, Mary Lou's house was an authentic repro-
duction of a classic Creole plantation-style home.
Painted with a black roof and matching shutters, the
home featured front and rear covered porches encased
with white wood railings. Pale pink flowering dogwood trees lined the walk to Mary Lou's double front
doors.

Whistling appreciatively, Sam looked around the
quiet interior of Mary Lou's gracious home. "The inside of this place sparkles," he acknowledged, noticing

how the Wedgwood gleamed inside the dining room hutch, as if Mary Lou had just washed it for company.

Fern touched a bowl of live Swedish ivy, her gaze lighting on other flower arrangements in the dining room. There was bearded lavender iris, dwarf yellow narcissus, tall peach tulips, pink baby's breath, and sweet-smelling hyacinths in yellow, purple, and blue.

Looking at the flower arrangements, Sam decided he liked Hurley's touch, but Mary Lou's even better. Her soothing ocean wall murals turned up, in miniature, around the switch plates making them seem to disappear. He wondered when she had developed the concept of painting around hardware. Thoughtfully, he sniffed a blue hyacinth, its star-shaped flowers tickling his nose. He decided right then to get some for Bailey's formal bulb garden in their front yard.

"Mary Lou's home is gorgeous," he noted to Bailey as he lightly swatted Fern's inquisitive fingers away from a plastic container of lemon wedges. "Sugar, why don't you go look at the flowers in the backyard for a minute while Mom and I organize the boxes?" Fern liked the idea on the spot. Smiling, she rushed out the back door.

Bailey followed Sam into Mary Lou's kitchen. "I've always liked Mary Lou's home," she said softly. "See how the varied flowers add depth, while the outlet and switch-plate murals add character?"

Disappointment swept through Sam unexpectedly. He had considered Mary Lou just one of Bailey's many women friends, someone only to smile at and to say a brief hello. He wished he had known this creative woman better. Being in Mary Lou's home for the first time made him wish he had spoken with her more than he had. "It's tough to imagine she's gone, a woman in her prime."

Sam's curiosity about Mary Lou's death increased the longer he stayed in her house. Like his wife, he wondered about the details behind the reason her friend died. As he unloaded Bailey's boxes in Mary Lou's clean kitchen, he noticed its lack of warmth, its lack of her presence. "I don't see how it's possible to know exactly why she did it," he said at length. "You said she never seemed sad or depressed, but maybe it was something too personal to discuss. Even with you."

Bailey shook her head. "I sat with Mary Lou in her kitchen the day before she died. We drank a pot of coffee, downed doughnuts, and plotted calorie-burning strategies. I can't believe it. I don't buy into her suicide."

"I hear you," Sam concluded. "A woman jumping ship in the middle of the day on a pleasure trip with her husband is unthinkable to me. Even though the act itself is a concrete, explainable act, the reasons behind the act are unexplainable—especially when there wasn't a note. I know why you're frustrated, but there's no way to discover the reasons now."

Being in Mary Lou's house the day before her death only confirmed what Bailey's instincts had shouted from the moment she first heard how Mary Lou died— something was terribly wrong. "What does instinct tell you, Sam? Be honest."

He did not miss a beat. "Instinct tells me Mary Lou's death doesn't jive with everything you've told me about her." Seeing Bailey's troubled expression, he asked, "What're you thinking?" His voice was carefully controlled and low, the skin on his powerful arms awash with scattered goose bumps. Precognition—and intimate knowledge of his wife—warned him his life was about to change in a big way.

Bailey looked him in the eye. "I want honor for Mary Lou."

Sam returned the look. "Tell me what you mean."

Bailey jammed her fingers through her straightened hair, trying to put words to her troubled feelings about Mary Lou. "This whole suicide mystery carries the burden of scandal. Scandal and honor are opposites, Sam. I want to understand why Mary Lou's public life was honorable, something completely opposite to the obvious confusion that was in her private life. Suicide was a cowardly way for her to die. Mary Lou never backed down from anything, Sam. It just doesn't make sense."

The power of Bailey's passion for Mary Lou scudded across Sam's emotions. He paused before speaking, considering his words carefully. "It's natural for you to want to know what went wrong. What happened to Mary Lou is tragic."

"What are you talking about, Daddy?" Fern asked as she entered the kitchen.

"We were remembering Miss Mary Lou, sugar."

Fern smiled sadly. "Me, too."

Opening her arms to her daughter, Bailey planted tiny kisses against the top of her head. "Let's finish setting up for the reception."

Her wits gathered firmly, Bailey instructed Sam to snap portable table legs into position on top of the lush green lawn. After the tables were in place, Fern covered them with linen tablecloths. Once the tables were covered, Bailey placed small clusters of tiny violets in

Fern's waiting palms. Almost reverent, Fern delivered the tiny bouquets into diamond-cut crystal vases. Between the vases, Bailey secured spots for the buffet dishes.

Proud of the final result, Sam surveyed his family's handiwork. "We've hardly been here an hour and we're almost finished," he observed. "You've got to be the most organized woman I've ever met."

Bailey beamed, glad she could present an elegant visual farewell to Mary Lou, a farewell her friends could enjoy and remember in a positive way. She wanted things to be perfect. Now that everything was in place for the funeral reception, she took a break. A fresh breeze skimmed across the backyard. The lilting sweet songs of birds drifted along the air, and their languid flight above Mary Lou's home was a pleasure for Bailey to see. Enticed to enjoy the birds' flight, she moved to Mary Lou's backyard bench swing. Taking Fern's hand into her own, she pulled her along with her to sit on the swing, taking in the tranquillity of the morning.

Sam ambled off the lawn to stand on the brick deck, a surface adorned with emerald-colored wrought iron chairs that nestled against matching tables. He directed his attention to the serene stillness found in Mary Lou's backyard. The view from the deck enchanted him. Like Bailey, Mary Lou had favored theme gardens to fill her spacious yard. There was a section of purple iris, pink azalea, assorted annuals, and purple roses. Aside from the theme gardens, peonies grew rampant along a picket fence, a faultless setting for the gazebo with its willow furniture centered on the lawn. The gazebo was a spot that invited gentle laughter while one sipped iced tea.

Sam looked around the spacious yard one more time, Bailey's skepticism echoing in his head. Confounded, he frowned, knowing his mind would not settle easily.

Minutes before the guests arrived at the Booker home, he stopped to speak with Bailey at the buffet table, where she stood eyeing her food display. Fern was in the rose garden, pressing petals against her nose. "This doesn't feel like the home of a terribly depressed person," he decided. "Look at all the details, tiny touches that show how much Mary Lou loved her home. I agree with you. Something isn't right."

Bailey smiled then and hugged him. "Thank you, Sam."

He hugged her back, glad she was more at ease. He tried to remember the last time he had told her the world meant nothing to him without her at his side, but he could not. He took it for granted that she'd always be with him. This sobering thought in mind, he embraced her face with his hands, kissing her lips with affection. "Bailey, I love the life we have together, the laughter, the fights, the making up. Everything. I especially love you for making me a father. What about having another child? Let's make a baby."

"Sam!" Bailey's eyes crossed his face to see if he was for real.

He laughed at her startled expression. "I'm serious," he assured her, gathering her up tight in his arms. On impulse, he lifted her into the air and swung her around.

Bailey squealed with delight. "But Fern is going on eight!"

"So what?" he challenged her as his palms slid down her sides to settle on her waist. "She'll love it."

Bailey threw her arms around his neck, excited yet appalled by his suggestion. "Maybe we can start tonight," she teased him, conscious of how the look he was giving her put a curl in her toes. As far as she was concerned, the night could not come fast enough.

Hours later Bailey listened as stiletto heels clicked against Mary Lou Booker's backyard deck. The distinct female sounds accompanied the hum of varied conversation in the well-dressed crowd. Dapper men grouped in heavy-voiced clusters near the gazebo. Elegant women monitored restive children, two of them adorable twin boys. The boys' rough play reminded Bailey of the continuous life thread that granted human beings immortality.

Vigilant of the proceedings, Bailey noted that both Mary Lou's and Hurley's parents were present. Mary Lou's parents, Mr. and Mrs. Perkins, seemed to function on automatic, their smiles reaching their eyes only when centered upon Cambria. Genial cohosts, Hurley's parents, the Bookers, greeted guests in tandem. Like the Perkinses, Bailey observed how they, too, shared a deep concern for Cambria, an obvious assumption from the careful way they tended her needs. Both sets of grandparents made certain Cambria received love and support.

Looking at Hurley, Bailey decided that if he needed help, he did not show it. Six feet tall, inky-skinned, and handsome, all Hurley's energy was focused on hosting the gathering, a feat he accomplished while looking marvelous in a double-breasted navy suit, an elegant backdrop to Cambria's classic navy dress.

It was Cambria who cornered the bulk of Bailey's concern. The child's cinnamon-colored skin matched her mother's, as did the shape of her oval face. Hazel eyes shone misty beneath pencil-slim brows. The child was as pretty as she was reserved.

Standing beside her father near the gazebo, Cambria slowly walked over to Bailey. "The food's good, Miss Bailey," she said shyly.

Keenly aware of Cambria's plight, Bailey struggled to keep tears from spilling down her cheeks. It hurt her to see the girl's valiant effort not to collapse into tears herself. "Thank you, Cambria," Bailey responded softly and sincerely. She smoothed an escaped tendril of wiry hair from the little girl's brow. "You're welcome to visit with Fern anytime you want."

Cambria's face became more solemn. "Thank you, Miss Bailey, but I can't come," she declined in a sad, polite voice. "Daddy says we're moving."

Surprised, Bailey asked, "During the summer?"

"No, after the reception." Cambria said angrily, Bailey noticed.

Bailey could not believe the sudden news of the Bookers' rapid departure. She had spoken with Hurley twice before the funeral to confirm menu details and buffet arrangements for the reception. He had never mentioned a move either time, making her wonder why he had kept the news a secret. She intended to ask him.

Bailey found Hurley in the kitchen at the sink, a

bottle of wine gripped solid in his right fist. He put
the green bottle down in order to give her a calculating
look. His black eyes were distant and cold.

"Cambria says you're leaving," she said, put out that
he had not told her himself. Although she saw Hurley
on rare occasions, Bailey expected open behavior from
him considering his request that she prepare food for
the funeral reception. While preparing the food had
helped Bailey work out her grief over Mary Lou's
death, she considered it a joint venture between herself
and Hurley.

It took Hurley thirty seconds to respond to Bailey's
statement. Unaccustomed to explaining his actions to
anyone, he took his time responding. When he opened
his mouth to speak, not a scrap of feeling traveled the
length of his tone despite the passion of his words. "I
can't stand this place. Every time I turn around I see
Mary Lou. On top of that, Cambria cries herself to
sleep. She spends most of her time with Mary Lou's
mother, Yolanda."

Hurley's revelation broke through Bailey's anger.
The image of Cambria crying herself to sleep made
her realize that Hurley may have been incapable of
giving his daughter the support she needed: his own
feelings seemed repressed. His response to let Cambria
cry until she was too exhausted to do it anymore was
troubling. Bailey hoped it was a temporary reaction to
Mary Lou's death. "I'm sorry."

Hurley laughed, a bitter sound in the emptiness of
Mary Lou's kitchen. The sound grated Bailey's nerves,
as did his brief assessment of her when she first ap-
proached him in the kitchen. Until then he had been
reserved yet polite in all his dealings with her.

Her eyes intent, Bailey watched Hurley pick up the wine bottle he set aside when she entered the kitchen. Watching him make his way to a vacant table outdoors, she wondered how he would manage a mourning child. His sudden move from the neighborhood, coupled with the certain change in Cambria's school in the final weeks of the term did not bode well for the child. Bailey was now more puzzled than ever about Mary Lou's death.

While Minette oversaw the food table, Sam entered the kitchen. "You look tired," he noticed, cognizant of Bailey's tiniest shift in mood.

"I'll be fine," she assured him, her eyes intense with emotion. She pressed nimble fingers to the small of her back, massaging the fatigued area. Standing on her feet for long hours preparing food had taken its toll. Sam moved behind her and placed his fingers over hers. She dropped her hands as he took over the massage.

Bailey welcomed his touch. More than simple love, she admired her husband's thoughtful ways and earthy spirit. His fingers against her back made her think of his body. She liked the way time had thickened his muscles into solid comfort. From his outward persona of protector to his supremely kind heart, Sam was all the man Bailey needed. She told Sam about her talk with Hurley.

He turned Bailey to face him then slipped his arms around her small waist. "Either he's keeping the pending move a secret because he doesn't want to detract from Mary Lou's final farewell, or because he doesn't want any questions about his actions, especially from well-meaning friends. He has that right."

While Bailey agreed with Sam, she was also plagued by the notion that something was very wrong with Hurley's behavior so soon after his wife's suicide. She found herself thinking back to things Mary Lou had said about him in the past. She was surprised when she realized Mary Lou had spoken more about Cambria than about him.

"It's Cambria I'm really worried about, Sam. She's in the final weeks of the school term. The sudden move following her mother's death won't do her any good. I'm surprised Hurley isn't moving more slowly. He's her father, yet he treats her as if she weren't his own flesh and blood. Have you noticed that he hasn't hugged or held her all day? I don't understand why."

Sam squeezed Bailey a little tighter. "Cambria is fortunate her grandparents are so attentive. They must see Hurley's distance from his daughter as you do. It might be the reason they keep her close, Mary Lou's mother in particular."

Sam lifted her chin in order to see Bailey's face more clearly. From the determined way she was pulling herself together he determined she was not finished with Hurley Booker, not where Cambria's future was concerned. "Have you looked at those pictures on the table in the hall?" he asked, wanting to change the subject.

"Not lately," she admitted.

Sam took over the job. "Go look."

The Bookers' long hallway, like the rest of the house, was adorned with flowers. The filled crystal vases added even more character to the stately home. Bailey spied the usual succession of baby pictures against the walls, each one sporting the dual dimples in Cambria's cinnamon-skinned cheeks. In miniature, a series of wedding photographs reflected the stunning vision of Hurley and Mary Lou. In every frame Mary Lou was radiant, an older version of Cambria.

For the second time that hour, several questions haunted Bailey about Mary Lou's death. What hateful personal demon had pushed the winsome woman over a final, morbid edge? What had driven her to suicide? Loneliness? But she'd had Hurley. Or had she? Bailey wondered what had happened to the happy couple in the hallway pictures. Was Hurley's attention to Mary Lou's favorite food, the flowers all over the house, and the final farewell in the home he had shared with his wife, a crafty, deceitful act?

Bailey shook her head to dispel her suspicious thoughts but doubt continued to plague her. Instead of being broken up over Mary Lou's death, Hurley appeared emotionally distant. It was as if what was happening around him was happening to someone else. Most of all, Bailey could not shake herself of Hurley's coldness toward Cambria. In contrast, Sam would never be so distant toward someone he loved. More than ever, Bailey wanted an answer to why Mary Lou chose death over life. Had Mary Lou's death been an accident, Bailey thought she may have found it easier to come to terms, but suicide? Instinct warned her that it just did not make sense.

For one thing, niggling doubts about Hurley's competence as a family man kept Bailey's mind spinning. What about his prominent position at the hospital, she wondered. Had Hurley's career ambitions taken precedence over his role as father and husband? If so, maybe it could be a reason why Mary Lou was unhappy enough to end her own life. Bailey returned to the kitchen, arriving in time to help Sam load fish onto a decorated serving tray.

"I'll be glad to get out of here," he stated gravely, feeling disquieted. "This is all too strange."

Without reserve Bailey agreed with Sam. "Another hour and we'll call it quits."

"Deal."

Leaving Sam in the kitchen, Bailey checked on Fern, her resident pro at serving beverages. "How are you holding up, Fern?"

"Fine," she answered. "We need more sugar cubes and cream, Mom."

"Sugar cubes and cream coming up."

"I like the lemonade," Cambria praised Bailey when she returned.

On impulse, Bailey gave the grieving child a heart-melting hug, the kind of hug that stops tears from falling, the kind that makes weighty burdens easier to bear. Cambria returned the squeeze tightly. Eyes closed, the child sunk her narrow body deep into Bailey's softer, fuller one. Bailey cooed sweet comfort to Cambria as the child pressed her face against Bailey's floral-scented breast. Then with a slight smile, Cambria walked swiftly away to stand beside her grandmother.

Someone gripped Bailey's shoulder, spinning her around. It was Sam. "Don't crack." He spoke each word distinct in her ear. "It's time to pack up."

Her face flushed, Bailey touched the hand on her shoulder with her cheek. "I can't believe they're moving," she said quietly.

"I don't blame Hurley," Sam admitted, glad he was

not in Hurley's shoes. He doubted he could stand his home either if Bailey weren't there to share it with him.

Bailey sniffed, her eyes still wet with tears. Dashing them away, she murmured, "I feel so sorry for Cambria."

Sam wiped away Bailey's tears with a handkerchief. He believed suicide did not happen suddenly or without warning. Maybe there were clues that even his perceptive wife had missed. Maybe Hurley knew more than he let on. Like Bailey, Sam wondered how solid Mary Lou's relationship had been with her husband. "Apparently few people really understood Mary Lou."

Bitter irony spilled into Bailey's voice. "Mary Lou rejoiced in life, Sam. She adored Cambria, her home, her mural art. I plan to find out why she died."

An ominous feeling seeped into Sam's bones. "You're not a detective, Bailey. Maybe we're making too much out of this."

Bailey's black-clad figure grew still. "Maybe not."

"Then be careful."

"Why?"

"Because the truth may damage everything good you thought you ever knew about Mary Lou."

Dessert for Twelve

Ambrosia
Snowball Cake
Vanilla Ice Cream
Apricot Tarts
Daiquiri Punch

Three

It was Thursday morning. Every third Thursday of the month, Bailey catered Minette's women's social group, Dessert Night, and this was one of those Thursdays. Dessert Night at Minette's ranked high on Bailey's list of regular jobs and it was one time where she mixed pleasure with business. Besides eating good food, the women's group discussed world issues, politics, career strategy, and relationships. Mary Lou often car pooled to the meeting with Bailey in order to help her set up, she reminisced. This month she would do it alone, a sobering prospect.

At nine that Thursday morning, Minette called Bailey from her desk at work. She had twenty minutes to spare before meeting with the Hospitality League, Providence Hospital's volunteer service organization. They would discuss fund-raising for the hospital. "Is everything running okay for Dessert Night?" Minette asked, her voice beautifully cultured and controlled.

Bailey knew quite well Minette had called simply to shoot the breeze, not run over last-minute decisions regarding Dessert Night. A stickler for details, Bailey seldom ran out of whack when it came to catering. She had discovered early on that repeat business relied heavily on efficient, timely service. "Everything is running smooth, Minette. I appreciate your call."

Swiveling her gray leather chair away from her cluttered desk, Minette forward-pedaled her elegant suede shoes in the direction of the light streaming in from an oversized rectangular window. The relaxed view eased her mind. Beyond the window, the landscape at the hospital's entrance lifted Minette's spirits when the pressure of work became too great. At that moment three gardeners from the hospital's service department were planting lavender, pink, and yellow impatiens. "Good. How is my godchild doing in school?"

Bailey's lips twitched up at the corners. "Besides talking too much in class, Ms. Einstein is doing great in school."

Minette laughed, a deep-throated, rich sound. She loved Fern's lively enthusiasm, what she considered an inherited gift from Bailey. "She gets her mouth from you and her brains from Sam," she teased.

Bailey laughed, too. "If you don't watch what you say, Minette, I'll bring a triple chocolate fudge cake tonight instead of ambrosia," she teased in return.

Minette instantly visualized a clear cake plate filled with one-hundred percent pure chocaholic delight. Her mouth watered. "You know how I hate to share your triple chocolate fudge cake with anyone. It's bad enough I ate nearly the whole cake by myself on my birthday. By the way, it's coming up in July."

Bailey chuckled. "As if you'll let me forget."

Minette ignored the good-natured sarcasm. "How is Sam?"

"Working nonstop as usual."

Looking down at her double-breasted suit, Minette turned wistful. "You're so lucky, Bailey."

"Why?"

Minette let out a long, audible breath, husky in tone. Sometimes talking to Bailey reminded her of what she had missed so far by making her career a priority. "You've got a lovely home, a beautiful daughter, and a darling husband."

"You can have those things."

"Part of me understands I can have those things. Another part of me is afraid to risk another long-term relationship."

Bailey understood Minette's reluctance to pursue a meaningful relationship—Minette couldn't put aside her failed marriage to Judd Ramsey, a man whose friends called him "Captain Player" because of his womanizing habits. "Your ex-husband chose the wrong means to deal with the fast way you reached the top of your field. He beat you. Most men would like your success."

Minette marveled at Bailey's on-target intuition. "I almost don't trust myself to try marriage again, Bailey."

"Why?"

Minette responded with staid calmness, glad to relieve her mind. "I'm still attracted to Judd."

Bailey spoke with quiet emphasis. "You were deeply in love with him once. You were married to him. You guys have a history together."

Minette's voice lowered. "There's more."

"What?"

Minette took a deep breath, letting it out slowly. "He stops by my town house sometimes to . . . talk."

Bailey was surprised. "I didn't know."

"I was too embarrassed to tell you."

Bailey used a matter-of-fact tone. "You're human. I have no right to judge what you do or who you spend your time with."

A husky quality entered Minette's voice. "That's not what I'm embarrassed to tell you."

Bailey held her breath a moment before asking, "What is it?"

"We don't always just . . . talk."

Bailey's face took on a dull red from anger. Until Judd began hitting Minette during their marriage, she had liked him. In the years when she knew him, she never expected he had a violent streak in him. When Sam talked to him about it, suggesting he seek therapy, both Judd and Minette had told the Walkers to mind their own business, which from then on, they had. "Did he hurt you?"

"Not since the divorce. But, that's not the reason I was embarrassed to tell you about Judd coming to see me sometimes."

Bailey was quick to reassure Minette. "We're friends. Tell me."

Minette's voice was so low, it was almost a whisper. "We still have sex. Usually it's in the evenings, when I'm often at home."

Bailey paused. "Minette, do you still want Judd?"

"Only with my body."

Bailey was shocked to discover that Mary Lou was not the only friend she had who led a double life. On the surface Minette and Mary Lou were very together women yet Bailey was quickly learning that they were adept at leading secret lives. With Mary Lou's death fresh in her mind, Bailey was determined to be strong and supportive with Minette. "It sounds to me as if your bond with Judd is still strong."

"I really want to break it off, Bailey. It's just that something about him appeals to the wild side in me. During our marriage Judd could be so lavish with his attentions that it was possible to lay aside problems. I kept hoping we could work out those problems. Bailey, Judd is a good sweet-talker. That's how he gets through the door."

Bailey could barely find words. She hated Judd for how he hurt Minette. How could she stay involved with him? she wondered. Instead of chastising her friend for her confession, she tried to keep the anger she felt out of her voice. "Was he coming by to try to work things out?"

"Yes. That's how we'd end up having sex. For a while it was good between us, like the early days of our marriage when we were everything to each other. Until his last visit . . ."

"Did Judd hurt you that last time?"

There was a heavy sigh through the phone. "He found out I was seeing someone."

Bailey wondered what other secrets Minette had. "You're seeing someone?"

Minette chose her next words with care. "Judd discovered the name of the man I'd been seeing."

Bailey discerned the odd catch in her girlfriend's voice. It told her Minette was omitting some aspects of her story. "Did Judd hurt you because you were seeing someone? Or did he hurt you because he knew who the guy was and was jealous?"

"Both."

"How bad?"

"Bad enough for me to know I was right to leave him."

Bailey was relieved. She believed Minette was basically sound in her judgment. She could not have made it to the top of her profession at such an early age if she had not been strong and ambitious, a natural leader. Bailey admired Minette's steady climb up the corporate ladder and considered her a good role model for Fern. "Does Judd stop by your house often?"

"No. Most of the time I simply don't answer the door. Eventually, he goes away."

"Why don't you move?"

"I like my house," Minette replied, sounding tired.

Bailey spoke firmly. "There are always other houses. There is only one you."

Minette's voice was thick and a little shaky. "If you keep talking like that, I'll start to cry."

Remembering Minette had a meeting in a few moments, Bailey put a hold on the sentiment until she could see her in person. "Are you still seeing the guy Judd was angry about?"

Minette's voice was hesitant. "Until recently."

"Are you okay?"

Minette sighed. "Not really."

Bailey did not like the weary note in her friend's voice. "We can talk about this tonight, when you have more time. Maybe things will work out," she said encouragingly.

"I don't think so."

"Why?"

Again Minette chose her words carefully. "The man I was seeing is . . . involved."

"Minette!"

"I know. It just . . . happened."

Bailey concentrated on the blanks in Minette's explanations. "He's married, isn't he?"

"Yes."

Bailey sighed. "Did you feel safe with a married man?"

Minette chuckled, a derisive sound. "Yes. I enjoyed his attention without worrying about the kind of commitment involved in a long-term relationship. I met my . . . friend, during a low point. Until recently I hadn't been able to see he was a lot like Judd. It just wasn't obvious to me at first. Even though I want to remarry someday, I first need to figure out why I'm attracted to men who aren't good for me."

"Counseling might help," Bailey suggested, hoping her friend would give it a try. Not only had Minette's husband had a penchant for other women toward the end of their marriage, he'd been physically abusive as well.

"It's on my mind," Minette admitted.

Bailey's voice was strong, yet velvet-edged. "Let me know how I can help and I will. I love you, Minette."

Minette sounded relieved. "I love you, too. Telling you this much is a load off my mind and my heart."

Warmth flooded Bailey's voice. "I'm glad. I'm here for you, girlfriend."

"What more could a woman ask for?" Minette joked, halfheartedly.

"The answer to Mary Lou's death," Bailey answered impulsively.

"My meeting isn't for another few minutes. Explain what's bugging you."

Bailey leaned back in her kitchen chair, thankful for the chance to voice her concerns about Mary Lou's family. "For starters, Hurley moved out the day after the funeral."

Minette backed her chair away from the window to her cluttered desk. Idly, she played with a steel paper clip. "I don't blame him."

Bailey sighed. "I understand his desire to move, Minette. It's the timing I don't get. Why jumble Cambria's life completely? And how did he find a new home so fast?"

Minette tossed the paper clip into a magnetic dispenser. As she did, she registered that with the funeral reception behind her, Bailey's mind was working overtime about the oddities surrounding Mary Lou's suicide. "A logical explanation is that they were looking for a new home prior to Mary Lou's death."

Bailey did not buy it. People were usually excited about purchasing a new home. In her experience, people told this kind of news to friends. "Then why wouldn't she mention to me they planned to move?"

"Obviously she didn't tell you everything." Minette reasoned.

In light of Mary Lou's suicide, Bailey was forced to agree, but she rejected Minette's idea. She did not believe Mary Lou would keep a house-hunting secret any more than she would change Cambria's school at the last minute. Both prospects were completely out of character. She sighed. "Mary Lou invited me to coffee the day before she died, Minette. I didn't have a clue she felt desperate."

Minette considered Bailey's point. "I do believe people have low moments, snatches of time when they feel indescribably depressed. Maybe Mary Lou received bad news the Saturday she died, news that made her desperate. Maybe she and Hurley were arguing and she jumped in a fit of passion. Whatever happened, I'm just glad Cambria was at her grandmother's house at the time."

Entertaining the image depicted by Minette, Bailey's fingers drummed an erratic tempo against the tabletop where she sat. "True. Only I don't buy into Mary Lou jumping overboard ship, because she was so crazy about Cambria. Mary Lou loved her, thought the world of her. She did everything she could to protect Cambria. She was a caring mother, not a depressed woman at all. I just don't get it."

Minette rifled a hand through her bangs, then instantly regretted the action. She had twelve minutes left before the Hospitality League meeting started. In order to repair the damage she had created with her hand, she pulled a mirror and comb from the bottom drawer of her ancient desk. "Maybe Mary Lou's death had something to do with Cambria," she fished.

"Or maybe it had something to do with Hurley," Bailey countered, thinking it more logical. After all, she thought, only Hurley had witnessed the suicide, something Bailey considered strange in itself.

Minette frowned. Because they were both health care professionals in the same hospital, she came in contact with Hurley a great deal. She had noticed nothing unusual in his behavior the Friday before his wife's death. A thinker, Hurley Booker performed his medical duties with his usual insight and detached professionalism. "You're making this all too complicated, Bailey," she decided. "Mary Lou is beyond help now."

Bailey pushed a tendril of hair off her forehead. "It's not Mary Lou I'm worried about. It's Cambria."

Minette returned the mirror to its proper place. She snapped the bottom drawer shut, wishing she could close Bailey's issue in the same way. She did not think anything good would come from stirring up Mary Lou's past. "Hurley will take care of Cambria."

Bailey patted her loafer-clad foot against the kitchen floor. "I hope so. Taking Cambria out of school so close to the end of the year is not a good measure of Hurley's judgment as a parent," she advised. In the past, Bailey knew Mary Lou was the primary caregiver. She hoped that Hurley's parenting skills would improve with time.

Staring at the ceiling, Minette leaned backward in her seat, thinking of Hurley, a workaholic like herself. "Hurley's passion is cousin to his ambition."

Bailey paused, not expecting the insight. "How would you know, Minette?"

"I work with him, remember?" she answered quickly.

The tense edge to her jaw indicated Bailey's frustration. "I think something kept Mary Lou from confiding her troubles to Hurley, if it's true he didn't know why she jumped." There had to have been hardship between them, she determined, thinking Mary Lou might destroy herself over an alarming vision of the future or some damning consequence of the past. Intuition told her that only a problem of terrible magnitude could make a woman like Mary Lou Booker leave her only daughter.

A brief wave of discomfort passed through Minette.

"The truth is, Bailey, we may never know what happened." Minette's intercom buzzed, indicating it was time for her meeting. "I need to run, Bailey. I'll meet you at my town house at six-thirty tonight. Use your key to let yourself in to set up the buffet."

Bailey glanced at her watch. "I'd best get cracking myself. See you tonight."

After speaking with her friend, Bailey washed her hands at the double sink, then set to work on the ambrosia. Pulling her trusty red mixing bowl from the pantry, she rinsed it out and swished it dry with a green checkered dish towel. Working with precision, she collected the oranges she needed for the creamy salad. Carefully, she peeled off the skins and stored them to make potpourri with Fern and Jordanna.

She sliced the peeled oranges into bite-sized pieces, spreading a quarter of them along the bottom of a crystal serving bowl. Snowy flakes of coconut were sprinkled on top of the oranges. Bailey capped the coconut with crushed pineapple. This done, she repeated the process, starting and ending with the oranges before she placed the crystal bowl in the refrigerator. To keep the ambrosia from drying out, she covered the bowl with clear plastic wrap.

Glancing at the clock, Bailey loaded the dishwasher and wiped the counters down. She had less than three hours before she had to pick up Fern and Jordanna from school. She pushed ahead to the snowball cake, another one of Minette's favorite confections because she liked the fresh coconut Bailey used.

Next on the menu came the apricot tarts, little goodies that were a snap for Bailey to make. All she needed were eggs, milk, sugar, cornstarch, salt, canned apri-

cots, and three-inch pie shells. When it came time to
serve them at Minette's she would squeeze out a decorative squirt of whipped cream.

Wiping down her work space, Bailey was ready to
make the vanilla ice cream. She needed sugar, cornstarch, salt, half-and-half, eggs, heavy cream, and vanilla. The electric mixer did all the work while she
creamed her water-wrinkled hands with cocoa butter.

Then Bailey pulled a memo pad from the counter
and a pencil from a cup by the telephone to list what
she needed to do at Minette's. Without Mary Lou present to share the set-up as they had done in the past,
she did not want to forget a single thing.

In the dining room at Minette's executive-styled
town house, Bailey perused a portfolio of artwork by
the renowned photographer Edith Stone. Miss Stone's
work was currently on display at the New Hope Township Institute of Fine Arts. The gallery had been es-
tablished by Minette's mother, Gladys Johnson, a
philanthropist. Bailey complimented Minette on her
mother's community work. "Your mother's vigor
helped to make New Hope a cultural mecca."

Minette lifted the color portfolio from Bailey's willing grasp. "I'm proud of her. People come from all
over the Bay Area to visit the lovely exhibits she spon-
sors at the gallery. She was ecstatic to acquire a showing of Edith Stone's work."

Bailey flashed a grin at the look on Minette's face.
She believed part of Minette's success in her career
stemmed from a desire to be a strong leader within
her own community like her mother. "I like the way

Stone portrays the black woman. She turns the common into the uncommon."

Minette nodded her head, understanding Bailey completely. "Stone can photograph an ordinary woman in such style, one can see the classic qualities of strength, endurance, and comfort. The exhibit is a major coup for Mom." Her expression earnest, Minette squeezed Bailey's hands, extremities enhanced with some of the same strength, endurance, and comfort depicted in Edith Stone's unique and powerful photography of common women doing everyday things—like cooking. "You sometimes remind me of my mother," she confessed.

Bailey laughed, her eyes twinkling at the compliment. "You're kidding?"

Minette was serious. "Like you, she successfully combined her work with her family."

Her eyes warm, Bailey spoke softly. "Your mother reminds me a little of Mary Lou."

Surprised, Minette asked. "How?"

"She's sincere in her quest of nature and art. Mary Lou was the same way. Like Mary Lou's work, your mother's work is a legacy of beauty."

Minette marveled at the comparison. "You're so insightful, Bailey. I don't believe I'd ever have considered the similarities between them. But, my mother isn't a literal artist the way Mary Lou was an artist."

"I disagree."

"On what?"

Bailey considered her view, then explained it. "Your mother designed the gallery based on a lifelong dream and a desire to leave beauty in the world. That's art. And another thing."

"What?" Minette prompted, intrigued.

"Gladys created you, a natural beauty," Bailey responded, her eyes smiling.

Minette pulled Bailey into her arms for a quick hug and squeeze. "You sure know how to boost a person's spirits."

Bailey squeezed Minette back, thinking her friend smelled divine in Wrappings perfume. Her friend also looked powerful and elegant in a tailored mauve pantsuit. Minette's persona combined brawny brains with electric energy to project the image of a woman who could gain attention by sheer presence alone.

In contrast, Minette thought Bailey looked soft and warm in a silky, above-the-knee mint dress. She was an alluring combination of sincerity and loving kindness. Her earth-mother qualities grounded those people around her, people like herself.

Thoughtful, Bailey said, "No one would guess you were a battered wife."

Minette scowled, remembering her stormy marriage to Judd, a man she had met in college where he majored in the arts and she majored in health care administration. While he was an ambitous sophisticate, she was a status seeker. "My brothers beat him up on my behalf the first time Judd . . . hurt me. After that I kept it a secret from the family. But a few of my friends knew."

In retrospect, Minette realized her and Judd's desire for material things had prevented them from enjoying life in the singular way Bailey did with Sam. She felt the Walkers' value system put people and feelings first, and maybe that accounted in part for their happiness. Minette and Judd had wanted everything their money could buy them. In the years they were married, they had acquired much in the way of material things, beginning with the spacious tri-level town house, where Minette now lived alone.

"One night he slammed my head into a wall so hard, I conked out," Minette recalled, angry all over again. "It was the last fight we had before I filed for a divorce. I wasn't sure I could take it anymore."

"I was glad you divorced him. I worried about you constantly."

"I know you were worried. It's why I tried keeping my marital life separate from our friendship. After the divorce, you assumed I wasn't seeing him anymore, which reduced your worries even further. I was too embarrassed to say I was still seeing him sometimes."

As Bailey listened to Minette, she graced the edges of the snowball cake with violet flower sprigs to provide an eye-catching ornament for the dessert table. The combination of purple and white on the cake plate reminded her of spring. She placed the violet-edged serving plate next to the fresh-smelling ambrosia. Once all the other desserts were in place on the table, Minette helped her pour the punch into a serving bowl. Beside the bowl were tiny glasses embossed with rosebuds. Meticulous as ever, Bailey adjusted the table decorations in order to make sure the table looked balanced. Minette's tall brass candelabrum added the perfect ambiance when combined with Bailey's peach-scented spiral candles.

"Everything looks marvelous as usual," Minette told her in a rush. She was a little sheepish now that she had bared her secret about Judd, because she valued Bailey's respect for her.

Aware of Minette's tension, Bailey put a hand on her left forearm. "You okay?"

Minette ran a smoothing hand across the table linen. "I'm feeling a little shy after my confessions."

Bailey chuckled. "One thing you've never been is shy."

A warmth spread through Minette at Bailey's smile. She relaxed. "It's not every day I confide something so raw about myself. Telling you about Judd this morning was . . . cleansing. Just getting the words out was a relief."

Bailey looked at her friend intently. "I'm not here to put you down. I love and respect you."

Minette inhaled a deep, unsteady breath. "I feel the same way about you. I just don't want your feelings to change about me because I've made some . . . mistakes."

Bailey studied Minette with a frank expression. "Are you still in love with Judd?"

"For a long time I was in love with him. I'm not anymore."

If love was not the pull for Minette to see Judd, Bailey believed there had to be something equally compelling for her to let him have access to her life after their divorce. "Was it just the sex?"

Minette closed her eyes briefly. When she opened them, they were solemn and clear. "It was at first. Most of my time revolves around the office, even my social events. I feel like I'm on my P's and Q's all the time. Judd can make me feel . . . uninhibited."

"I can understand how he could make you feel freer. He's always liked new experiences, new foods, adventure. On the other hand, you're very goal-oriented, image-conscious, focused. Together you both were able to find a balance, the reason you married. I imagine all that emotion mixed with compatible sex and smoldering love is a powerful combination."

Minette grimaced. "Until I started making more money than him during our marriage."

Bailey never had understood Judd's problem with Minette's salary. As long as it went toward mutual goals, she did not believe it mattered who made what. "His contracting business is successful."

Minette snorted, recalling the subject of many an argument between her and Judd. The year before they divorced had been a bitter one. "His contracting business doesn't have comparable . . . perks."

"What do you mean?"

Minette reeled off a few of the benefits of her profession. "A gas allowance, paid country club dues, paid Rotary Club fees, a one-thousand-dollar table at the hospital's annual society fund-raiser, car insurance, life insurance, health insurance . . . the list goes on. Judd had a problem with those perks, especially the country club."

"Why the country club?" Minette was especially close-mouthed about her dealings with Judd after he told the Walkers to stay out of his marital business. They had, considering Minette able to decide what she could or could not live with in a man.

"Image. Country-club status invokes images of wealth and privilege. Even though Judd owns his own business, he comes home dirty every day from his job sites. I come home dressed to the nines and smelling like roses. The differences grated on Judd during our marriage."

"Hitting you was wrong no matter what." Imagining such an action made Bailey cringe.

Minette shuddered visibly, acknowledging her part in the domestic violence. "He knows he was wrong. He was always very sorry afterward. When I listened to his sweet talk, I would take him back. Things would get better until he had an especially trying day or I had an especially successful one."

"Judd was out of control."

"So was I."

Bailey appreciated Minette's honesty. "What's different now?"

"Mary Lou's death."

The answer was unexpected. "Did Hurley abuse Mary Lou?"

Minette paused. "I don't believe he would . . . hurt her the way Judd hurt me. No."

Unconsciously, Bailey frowned. "Then how does Mary Lou's death make you feel different about Judd?"

Minette's expression turned bitter. "Not just Judd. Men period. Me period."

Bailey felt like Minette was holding back because whatever she said was measured with care. "I still don't get it."

"I'm saying that Mary Lou was a dreamer and a fighter. At our women's groups she would always say she wanted to leave something beautiful in the world when she died. She left her art and her daughter. She fulfilled her dreams even though she died young."

"You've fulfilled your dreams too," Bailey insisted to Minette. "You dreamed of being a hospital administrator. Now you're the chief administrator in the largest medical facility in New Hope."

"I'm not a fighter," Minette answered.

Bailey did not believe that for an instant. "You have to be a fighter to make it to the top of your field."

"That's not the kind of fighting I'm talking about, Bailey. I'm talking about fighting with and for my emotions. Even though I divorced Judd, I still hadn't finished with him. I bet Mary Lou wouldn't . . ."

By focusing her friendship on Minette's basic good nature and solid achievements Bailey now discovered she had not really dwelled on the negative aspects of her friend's personality. After talking so frankly with Minette, she could see she had behaved the same way in her relationship with Mary Lou. Bailey also realized she had accepted each woman's friendship unconditionally, on whatever terms each friend was able to give. As a result, she had glossed over the negatives between the friendships because the positives in their relationships were strong and sincere.

"If you thought she was a fighter, why do you think Mary Lou did it?" Bailey asked softly.

"I never thought about her death that way," Minette said after a thoughtful pause.

"Well, I have," Bailey admitted. "I agree that she never backed down from anything. It's why I have a problem with her suicide. She was honest with her emotions. I can't imagine her keeping something inside her that was so dreadful she could no longer stand to live. She liked painting murals. She loved her daughter."

"She was always talking about Cambria," Minette responded.

"I remember. And you know what?"

"What?"

"I don't remember her going on and on about Hurley. It was always her art, or her daughter, or her mother, or something. Whenever she talked about Hurley, it was in general terms, like the weather."

Minette shrugged. "They may not have had a good marriage."

"I wonder. To tell you the truth, Hurley puzzles me."

"Why?"

Bailey considered what she knew about Mary Lou's husband. "On the one hand, he's a strong man in the community. He runs a successful medical practice. He lavished his wife and daughter with expensive things. Instead of acting ashamed of the way Mary Lou died, Hurley opened his home to host the funeral reception. He used flowers from Mary Lou's gardens to liven any room guests might enter."

Minette's expression was rapt. Bailey's intuition had always been keen, making her impressions valued. "What's on the other hand?"

"His attitude."

"What about it?"

Bailey thought back to the funeral reception. She recalled the coldly furious way he had responded to her question about moving right away. "He's remote."

Minette lifted her right shoulder in a shrug. "In my experience as a hospital professional, I know that people express grief in varied ways. It could be shock."

Bailey was not completely convinced. "That's probably part of it. The other part of it is him. The few times I ever ran into Hurley he was cool and impersonal. What is he like to work with?"

Minette fired off a response. "Analytic. Perceptive. Knowledgeable. His work is respected. His opinions sought-after."

"Is he patronizing?"

"Cynical is more like it."

Talking with Minette clarified one of the misgivings she had about Mary Lou and Hurley. "Mary Lou was as warm as Hurley is cold."

Thinking about herself and Judd, Minette's expression grew taut. "I'm sure they must have had some point between them where they balanced."

Bailey listened to Minette with the vague sensation that something was amiss. Minette's body language was tense again, the way it had been when they first began talking. Bailey decided Minette had probably had enough soul searching for one day. "You may be right."

"I'm glad we talked," she admitted, effectively shifting their conversation.

"So am I." Minette's grin was more than a little forced, Bailey noticed.

Minette voiced a main concern. "I thought you'd be . . . upset with me."

Bailey used her voice and eyes to reassure Minette of their friendship. "I care about what happens to you. If I thought you were a negative person I would never have asked you to be godmother to my child. You've been good to Fern. And to me." When Bailey finished speaking, she extended her arms to Minette, who went into them with a long and eloquent sigh.

Comforted by Bailey's embrace, Minette closed her eyes, inhaling the appealing scents around her. Her senses alert, she focused on the smell of fresh coconut, apricot-touched pastry, and recently brewed European coffee. She thought it was wonderful to know Bailey, the most fantastic cook she had ever met. Most important to Minette, Bailey was her dearest friend.

Four

Minette greeted the Dessert Night guests as Bailey took one last look at the decorated buffet table in the dining room. All the fresh food was in place. Soft jazz music played in the background. Feeling satisfied with the food display, Bailey lit the peach candles before joining the rest of Minette's friends: Rachel, Iris, Joanne, Faith, Simone, Pearl, Audri, Lita, and Willow. The normal count was an even dozen when Bailey, Minette, and Mary Lou were counted. All of the guests were businesswomen in New Hope or members of the same health club. They found the Thursday night meetings a fun and relaxing respite from their daily lives.

As usual, for Dessert Night, Lita was the first guest to peruse the confection-adorned dining room table. Lita, a cappuccino-and-cream-colored woman, owned My Girlfriend's Closet, a clothing resale boutique. Her move toward the dessert table cued the rest of the women to do the same. After the initial hugs and kisses, the loading up of dessert plates and punch cups, all eleven ladies gravitated to Minette's living room, decorated in the pastel shades of lavender, lemon, and lime. The carpet was so pale a gray, it looked white in bright light. Three full-sized couches cut the large room into manageable bits. Floor-to-ceiling, doubleswagged valances in apricot provided a formal flair, a flair offset with subtle edgings in celadon.

The first topic of conversation at Dessert Night was Mary Lou.

"What was the funeral like, Minette?" asked Iris, an architect. She had not been able to attend the funeral because she was out of town and the reception had been by invitation only. Of the women's group, only Minette and Bailey attended the funeral and reception: Minette as the Providence Hospital representative, Bailey as the caterer.

"It was beautiful," Minette answered. "Hurley did a great job with the arrangements." She sounded both pleased and proud, something Bailey considered odd since Minette was Hurley's coworker and not a relative or close friend.

"I can't believe she's dead," drawled Joanne. Texas born, Joanne was a consumer test market analyst.

Willow, a corporate attorney, was visibly upset. "No one can believe she's dead," she said, her normally clipped voice a bit frayed around the edges. "I always thought she was stable. It's shocking to realize she concealed her misery so well."

Bailey realized her mouth had dropped open slightly when Faith, a bank manager said, "I wouldn't mind consoling the good doctor." Her voice was silky smooth and ever so sly.

"Faith!" Minette scolded, her face outraged.

Faith did not look at all embarrassed by her comment. "Well, it's true," she continued. "Hurley Booker is the blackest, finest man I've ever met. Never a hair out of place and always a smile on his face."

Pearl spoke up, her voice prim but not proper. "He

and Mary Lou sure made a good-lookin' couple."
Kansas-raised, Pearl was a travel agent.

Lita stopped licking vanilla ice cream off her silver
teaspoon. "I heard Mary Lou was seeing someone,"
she mentioned with a lilt that hinted of gossip.

Audri, an accountant, was offended by the tone and
by the remark. Her voice was indignant. "Mary Lou
wouldn't do that, Lita."

Faith raised her brows. "People have affairs all the
time, Audri. Don't be dense."

Simone, a town council member, edged into the conversation. Her hearty voice rang with strength. "Ap-
pearances lie, Audri. We don't have a clue about the
true nature of Mary Lou's relationship with Hurley."

"But she seemed so happy!" Iris blurted out, her
voice tinged with incredulity and wonder at what had
happened to Mary Lou. A heated rumble crisscrossed
the room, reminding Iris that Mary Lou jumped ship.
"Okay, so apparently she wasn't happy," she amended.
Turning to Lita, she asked. "Who was she seeing?"

Lita's voice was loaded with gossipy innuendo.
"You can best believe I tried to find out. A customer
at my boutique saw Mary Lou in a tight clinch with
some guy in San Francisco. The man was wearing a
baseball cap and a light jacket. But one thing was for
sure, the fella wasn't ebony-skinned like Hurley. All
my source could tell me was that the guy was light,
lighter than Mary Lou."

Her eyes wide, Pearl nearly dropped her apricot tart.
"Who is your source?"

Bailey watched as Lita shook her head, relishing the
drama. She suspected Lita never liked Mary Lou that
much. She had heard Lita call her uppity since Mary

Lou never frequented the resale boutique. "Unh-unh. My source is a big customer. No way will I run the risk of losing her business to gossip. I will tell you, though, that I trust her word."

Bailey did not like the way Lita relished speaking ill of the dead. The only good she found in Lita's revelation was in discovering Mary Lou did indeed lead a life of which she'd had no inkling. "I wonder why Mary Lou would date someone, when she seemed secure in her marriage with Hurley?"

Lita selected another slice of snowball cake, enjoying center stage. Picking off several pieces of toasted coconut with a damp finger, she licked them off with a flick of her tongue. "Beats me. I could hardly believe it myself."

Rachel, a beauty salon owner said, "We all keep secrets, especially when they involve taboo relationships. I don't blame her for not telling us. We're a bunch of talkers. I guess she couldn't risk telling even one of us about her affair."

Faith joined the conversation, her smooth voice sounding conspiratorial. "Besides, taboo relationships can be exciting. Maybe Hurley was away from home so much, Mary Lou was bored. It happens."

Although the idea did not sit well, common sense told Bailey that Faith was right. "I don't like talking about Mary Lou like this when she isn't here to defend herself."

"Bailey's right, ya'll," Joanne cut in. "Why bring up this kinda garbage now?"

"Because Mary Lou killed herself, that's why," Lita argued.

"I want to know what really made Mary Lou Booker

tick," Faith agreed softly. "Obviously, we didn't know her as well as we all thought we did."

"I always considered her a private person," Audri admitted.

Lita snorted. "Sneaky was more like it."

"We all bring up the special men in our lives at some point, but not Mary Lou. I figured she thought she was in a class by herself being married to a doctor," Lita argued.

Iris gasped at Lita's nerve. "You're saying she thought she was better than us?"

"Yeah."

Willow couldn't believe what she was hearing so soon after their friend's death. "Minette doesn't talk about men either. Does that make her sneaky or snobbish?"

Lita tsked. "Of course not."

Faith cut in. "Unh huh. Do you really mean that or are you just saying it because Minette is one of your regular clients at the boutique? Lord knows she buys clothes like some people drink a cold glass of water in July—fast and for one time only."

Minette glared at Faith.

Lita cocked her head to the side and scowled at Faith, too. "I'm saying Mary Lou never bothered to invite us over. I thought she was moody."

"An artist," Iris suggested.

Bailey thought only weddings brought out the best and the worst between friends because of the stress involved. Now she added funerals to the concept.

"Bull," Lita countered. "She was stuck up."

Bailey raised her hand in the halt position as she spoke out with firm authority. "My grandmother once told me that no matter how hard rain beats a leopard's skin, it can't wash out its spots." Although there had been times when Mary Lou was moody, she had always been a real friend.

Lita rolled her eyes and tsked. "What in the world are you talking about?"

Bailey's face was austere, her manner brooking no argument. "I'm talking about Mary Lou's basic goodness. Nothing can change that, not even a mistake."

Willow cleared her throat. "Bailey is right. I propose we move on to a less emotional issue. Like politics," she said with a nervous laugh.

That comment broke the tension and Bailey relaxed a bit. She had found out too much about Mary Lou that was unexpected, but oddly, she had not learned enough. She still did not know what event had caused her death.

"I consider America's Fund, a political action committee, a worthy topic," Willow continued.

"I've heard it's patterned after Emily's List," Pearl commented, noting everyone present was shifting gears. Although there were heated debates during Dessert Night, they never discussed something as personal as the death of someone close, nor had they behaved in such an ugly way to each other—as Lita and Faith had been doing with their innuendo and insults. Even though Mary Lou had quirks, Pearl reasoned, she was still a victim of a tragedy.

As it was the first time Simone had heard of America's Fund, she asked for more details. The topic was proving to be a satisfactory diversion from the subject of Mary Lou Booker's secret life.

"The organization is indeed patterned after Emily's

List, a political action committee dedicated to raising money for female Democrats," said Rachel. She spoke around a mouthful of snowball cake.

"Political action committees, or PACs, help members reach people outside their own voting districts," said Simone. She was tucking away the moist apricot tarts, delicious treats she intended to order from Bailey in two weeks for her office potluck.

"In a way, our women's group is an action committee," Minette noted. "I don't believe we've ever ended our session without deciding on something progressive and good to do within the community."

"She's right," Rachel agreed. "Only I'd never thought of it that way until now."

Neither had Audri. "Does America's Fund work the same way as Emily's List?" she asked, sipping punch.

"Pretty much," Simone answered. "Only America's Fund isn't exclusive to women. It's a fund-raising resource for minority leaders of both sexes, men and women headed toward public office."

"I've heard only good things about it," Iris noted. "I like the organization's versatility. Not only does it promote minority political leadership, it promotes urban renewal and small business development," she added. "Speaking of small business, Bailey, why don't you open a café? You could make a killing from your desserts alone."

"She's right," Rachel said. "Our group often discusses the need to promote women in business. We could start by promoting you."

Bailey shrugged, dismissing the idea. "A small business outside the home would be demanding, Rachel. I like being accessible to Fern."

"The business doesn't need to be all that big," Faith reasoned. "It could be a small coffee shop."

"I like working at home," Bailey told her.

"Stick-in-the-mud," Minette grumbled under her breath. Much of Bailey's referrals came from her. Bailey declined some of the potential clients in order to keep her business manageable.

Bailey rolled her eyes, then protested. "I'm not a stick-in-the-mud, Minette. I simply don't want to give up anything I have going in my life that works."

"I heard that," Audri commented. "If Bailey is happy, let her be. Now, let's get back to America's Fund before another argument breaks out. What else do you know about it, Willow?"

"It encourages people to enter politics. Even if it means involvement only through the voting polls," she answered.

"True," Minette added. "Organizations like America's Fund or even our women's group can play a key role in getting other women, like Simone, into upper-level political offices . . . or small business." She directed the last part of her statement to Bailey. Silently bolstered by everyone present except Bailey, Minette continued. "There are eleven of us right now in Dessert Night," she ascertained. "Each one of us plays a key role in the New Hope business community in the same way that America's Fund plays a key role in the political community. We can provide you with seed money to expand, Bailey."

"I agree," said Willow. "It appears to me your objection to expansion is leaving your home for long hours at a time. Correct?"

"Correct."

"Then develop an alternative to the restaurant angle," Willow suggested.

Intrigued, Bailey asked, "Like what?"

Willow temporarily placed her empty plate on the table, planning to load it up later with more treats. "You can develop recipes for specialty restaurants."

Bailey had never considered the idea. "Are you serious?"

"I am," Willow confirmed. "My aunt Cordelia talks often of opening a specialty café. She's thinking of serving Cajun food with an emphasis on gumbo recipes. She might be willing to pay someone to research and develop recipes for her menu."

Smiling, Minette liked the idea.

So did Joanne, who adored Cajun food. "You love perfectin' unusual recipes, Bailey. I don't know how many other small businesses are interested in that type of service, but I can run a test market search for you," she offered, enthused by the suggestion.

Bailey warmed as well. The more she thought about the recipe research and development angle, the more she liked it. Her grin ran around the room like a grass-fire.

Feeling good, as if they had reached a mountaintop together, the eleven women toasted in celebration of good things to come. The sound of the doorbell ringing interrupted their camaraderie.

"I wonder who that could be," Minette muttered on her way to the door, thinking her women's group needed a new name now that they were expanding the group's focus by offering seed money; she also liked the idea of supporting a woman like Simone in a national political office. Minette was so filled with purpose that she opened the door without checking the peephole first. "Judd," she gasped, surprised to find him standing outside. Lightening-quick, she slammed the door in his freckled face, but not before he jammed a booted foot in the door's crack.

Adrenaline pumping hard through her body, Bailey stood suddenly, ready to back Minette up in any way necessary. While it was not known to every woman in the room that Minette was still seeing Judd, it was common knowledge that their divorce had not been friendly.

Taking their cue from Bailey's warrior-woman stance and fierce expression, every woman in the suddenly hushed town house prepared for hand-to-hand combat against Judd. Shoes were donned in hand quicker than green beans being snapped. Overstuffed purses were hefted like thick slabs of frozen beef while everyone stared at Judd Ramsey as he pushed his way inside.

Judd was five-feet-ten-inches tall. Red hair crowned a narrow-shaped head, home to bushy brows, short, scanty lashes, and a barely-there mustache. Assorted-sized freckles scattered his yellow-brown face. His reckless smile could ignite a beach bonfire, it burned so bright. Dressed in expensive rugged-style clothes, he wore tan leather trail boots, snug-fitting light blue jeans, and a vanilla-colored cable-knit sweater. He looked every bit the reformed bad boy. In one swift glance he realized he'd picked the wrong night to make a surprise visit to Minette. He liked the challenge she presented, the main reason he kept showing up on her doorstep uninvited.

Spitfire mad at his interruption of the women's

group, Minette folded her arms across her breasts, suddenly very tired of Judd's sporadic visits. For the first time in a long while she was not in the least bit charmed by the handsome and crooked smile he tried to use in a way to disarm her. Much to her intense pleasure, Minette discovered her ex-husband's most devastating smile was not working its magic on her emotions tonight. "What do you want, Judd?" she demanded, breathing hard from embarrassment. Even though she found him attractive, she was seeing it from an objective standpoint: another private delight. She worked next on salvaging her image with her Dessert Night guests. She could only imagine what Lita would gossip about her at My Girlfriend's Closet after listening to her bad-mouth Mary Lou.

Minette worked hard on her public image, one that cultivated a blend of refined voice and strong leadership capped off with elegant clothes. Judd was the only man she had ever known who could make her turn primitive in an instant, leaving her inhibitions in the dust. She vowed to stay in control this time. Her eyes threw daggers at him.

Judd was delighted with the challenge. Chuckling softly he leaned against Minette's doorjamb, sizing her up. The way his eyes roved all over her face before resting on her mouth let every woman in the room see how much he wanted to kiss her cinnabar-painted lips. His hands even gravitated toward her, as if they had a will of their own and no other choice but to run over the familiar curves of his ex-wife's body. He had always liked her body, from the sleek and smooth cap of her hair to the supple soles of her feet.

Bailey noticed how Minette was breathing hard at

Judd's leisurely, insolent perusal. Her lips were parted and moist. Her hands were on her hips. Her head was thrown back while she studied him right back, giving as good as she got. Bailey had a hard time telling if Minette's body language was all anger or anger mixed with sexual excitement.

Judd did not have a hard time assessing Minette's body language. He could tell by the rough way she breathed that she was mad enough at him to scream the house down, an innate wildness that coincided with his own renegade spirit. In the past, such anger on her part had led to rousing, rip-roaring sex between them. Anger only fueled their passion. His body hard with torrid memories, Judd licked his lips, then waggled a blunt-tipped finger in Minette's livid face. "I came to talk."

"No."

Roguish, wicked laughter rumbled up from Judd's flat stomach as he watched Minette's temper fly higher and higher. The air between them crackled and popped as their past silently challenged their present for a stake in the future. He wanted one; she did not. Had they been alone he would have kissed her, a prelude to sex and his antidote to all their troubles. In the bedroom their problems had always ceased to exist.

Minette raked her eyes across Judd's body with the feeling she wanted to do it some harm. For the first time since their divorce, she saw him as the bitter and spoiled man he had become instead of the loving man she married. Having her friends present helped her see him clearly, a vision that effectively severed the sexual appeal for him that had lingered long after their divorce.

Stark relief swept through Minette. The silent, palpable, and unanimous support of her girlfriends convinced her to stay strong in the face of Judd's intense vitality. With her right fist poised to punch the scoundrel right smack in his scanty-lashed eye, she said coldly, "Get out."

The frigid shift in Minette's attitude made Judd forget they were not alone. His entire mind zeroed in on the woman before him. Muscling his unwelcome way further inside the gray-tiled foyer, he kicked the door shut behind him. He hated Minette ordering him around—unless it was in the bedroom.

"Watch out, Judd," warned Lita as she unsnapped dangling scarlet rings from her ears. "If you plan on staying, it's gonna get ugly in here." Minette was not just her hostess, she was her friend. Lita intended to help.

With her hands on her hips, Minette glared at Judd for all she was worth. "Lita's right, Judd. Leave now or deal with the police." She was feeling strong, invincible, proud of her decision to give him the ultimate boot.

While he made up his mind, Judd ignored every woman in the electrified room except for one. "I miss you, baby," he crooned, his voice smooth as honey. "I need to talk to somebody, and well, you're the best listener I know. We did have some good times together, baby. Come on. Let's talk. Just for a minute. Five minutes."

Contempt compressed Minette's eyes into narrow slits. "The last time I stepped outside to talk with you, Judd, you wound up knocking me to the ground."

Startled gasps went around the living room. Now

everyone knew exactly why Minette's divorce from
Judd had not been friendly. The women edged closer
to their friend, ready to pounce on Judd. Bailey held
a cordless telephone in her left hand, ready to either
bash Judd with it or call the police—whichever was
most necessary. Like every other woman present, she
was poised for action.

When Judd lifted his left hand in Minette's direction,
no one in the room waited to find out his intention.
Faith smacked the back of his head with a lavender
moiré pillow from the couch. Pearl fired pepper spray
at his chest in a one-time warning. Iris wielded her
blue suede purse like a brick weapon. Bailey punched
the first two digits of the 911 emergency line.

Whirling to face the contemptuous crowd of eleven
ladies now lining his exit to the open front door, Judd
saw clearly the fire end of someone's cigarette. It was
primed to burn a quick little hole into his body. Feeling
outnumbered, he lost the edge on his bravado. "Call
your she-wolves off, baby girl. I'll go."

What Judd lost in bravado, Minette gained in self-
esteem. "Do me a favor, will you? Stay gone this
time." Her face, like her tone, was full of contempt.
With her right hand she signaled for Bailey not to complete her call to the police.

At Minette's decisive action, expression, and tone,
Judd felt the sharp pang of regret. In the past she had
loved him, fought him, and cursed him. Never had she
spied him with such blatant scorn. The scorn cut
through his ego, severing his hold on her as surely as
any blade.

His eyes dark and unreadable, Judd turned to leave.
As he walked to the door, half a dozen moiré pillows

bounced off the back of his head. He neither ducked nor looked back, making every woman present wonder if perhaps their good friend was free at last. For Minette's peace of mind, Bailey hoped it was so.

Supper for Six

Stuffed Crab
Pork Rice
Peach Salad
Lemon Pound Cake
Sangria Punch

Five

It was Friday, Bailey's favorite day of the week because it started the weekend. But this particular Friday would be even more special because Jordanna was sleeping over. Bailey enjoyed the prospect of preparing a feel-good meal for her family and Fern's guest. Dressed in jeans, loafers, and a cotton top, she started dinner preparation with the lemon pound cake. Methodically, she pulled from the appropriate places lemon, butter, eggs, milk, flour, baking powder, baking soda, and sugar.

Humming the old seventies Tyrone Davis hit tune *Turn Back the Hands of Time,* Bailey reminisced about Mary Lou. Although she had been a serious and funny woman, Bailey realized Mary Lou had also been tormented and dishonest. She didn't know if she was more distressed by the revelations of the night before or that Mary Lou did not trust her enough to confide in her. The desire for Bailey to understand the reason Mary Lou died grew stronger with each passing day.

Trying to manage her sad thoughts by using her time productively, Bailey focused on the comforting task at hand, making food for her loved ones. In a yellow mixing bowl she creamed the sugar with the butter. Once the mixture was fully blended, she added the freshly grated lemon peel and squeezed lemon juice. In a separate glass bowl she combined the dry ingredients. Pushing the two bowls aside, she wiped down the tiled counter and washed the measuring tools.

After clearing her work space, Bailey combined the contents of the dry bowl with the contents of the creamed bowl. Using a hand-held electric mixer, she whipped the lemon pound cake batter until it crested the top of the mixing bowl. It didn't take long to lightly flour and grease a ten-cup fluted cake tin. Once the pound cake was in the oven, she quickly cleaned her work space for the next item on her dinner menu, peach salad.

Systematically, she gathered the vital ingredients for the salad: honey, grated ginger root, lemon juice, lemon peel, salad oil, mixed greens, peaches, and walnuts.

Feeling more at ease, she began humming. Soon, she was singing loudly as she belted out Billie Holiday's forties classic hit, "God Bless the Child." More feeling than talent lent the song its power as Bailey sang while she worked:

> Them that's got shall get
> Them that's not shall lose
> For the Bible says
> And it still is news

Bailey's grandmother once told her that people got what they deserved in life based upon the way they conducted themselves—good or bad. If this was true, Bailey wondered what Mary Lou had done to deserve the painful way she died. Winding the song down with

one more refrain, cold determination gripped Bailey.
Discovering Mary Lou had led a secret life, one in
which she had engaged in an affair only strengthened
Bailey's curiosity.

Her mind as methodic as her hands, she considered
the events of the night before, when Judd had brought
his handsome, arrogant self into Minette's women's
group. While Minette had talked trash to Judd, Bailey
noticed, her eyes had also raked his clothes straight off
his reportedly freckled fanny. Thinking of Minette's
ongoing relationship with Judd made Bailey furious.
How could such an intelligent woman put up with such
abuse? In order to soothe her nerves, she concentrated
on the job at hand, preparation of the pork rice, a dish
Fern was not crazy about because it relied heavily on
spices for flavor. Jordanna, like Sam, loved the spicy
pork bits in the rice.

By the time she had finished making the rice dish,
Bailey was feeling better. She moved on to one of
Sam's favorite foods: stuffed crab. Smiling, she anticipated the way his mouth would water over the entree.
The crab took a bit more time to prepare than the rice;
however, she considered the look on Sam's face worth
the effort. All Bailey needed was blue crab, homemade
seasoned salt, pepper, butter, scallions, celery, garlic,
cooking wine, and bread crumbs.

In a huge pot she boiled the crabs until they turned
red, then drained them onto paper towels. Once the
crabs cooled, she cracked the legs and underbelly, careful to keep the outer shell in tact while she scraped it
clean of waste and meat. She sautéed the scallions,
celery, and garlic. After five minutes she added the
salvaged crab meat, bread crumbs, wine, and season-

ings to her sauté pan. The resulting mixture was pressed into the crab backs, which she dotted with butter. She browned the entree in the oven for fifteen minutes.

Fern helped Bailey set the dinner table. Knowing Jordanna was coming for dinner, she prepared enough food for six adults in order to make sure there was enough for second and third helpings. For a small girl, Jordanna possessed a big appetite, the reason she was so pleasingly plump.

With a successful dinner behind them and only a minimum of food left over, Sam settled the girls into Fern's bedroom for the night while Bailey cleared the dishes from the table. When he returned to the kitchen wearing sweat pants and a T-shirt, he helped her wash the last of the plates. When these were dried, the couple sat on barstools at the counter.

"Tell me more about what happened at Dessert Night," Sam suggested. When Bailey told him about Minette still seeing Judd after their divorce, disdain flooded his face. He didn't believe a man ever had good reason to hit a woman. "I don't see why Minette put up with him."

Understanding his disbelief, Bailey heaved a sigh. "Those fists of his left a bold mark on Minette's self-confidence. I bet it's why she's so obsessed with finding a good man. Until then she surrounds herself with women friends; hence, a Dessert Night. She's healing."

The subject of troubled friends reminded Sam of the Bookers. "Did you talk about Mary Lou?"

A muscle flickered in Bailey's jaw. "Yes. We decided that no one really knew her. I thought I did."

Sam calmly voiced his opinion. "I don't believe it's possible to know anyone completely. We've been married ten years, yet you still surprise me from time to time. You've known Mary Lou for only three years. Maybe she didn't want to trouble you with her real problems."

Nagging doubts about Mary Lou's death fluttered inside Bailey's mind like lit candles on a birthday cake. She wanted to help Sam understand how it had been between her and Mary Lou. "I believe time between women friends is different from time spent between women and men. I think women friends I know cut down to the heart of a relationship a lot faster than men and women can."

A deep-throated, manly chuckle sprung from Sam's dark, handsome lips. Throwing his wife a teasing look, he earned his thick-muscled thigh a less than dainty smack from Bailey. She liked the way his chuckle turned into an actual laugh at her action, the warm sound of his voice adding to his flagrant masculinity. She loved it when he laughed like he did just then, a laugh reserved exclusively for her.

"You sound like a female chauvinist," he teased.

Bailey fixed him with a sizzling look that let him know exactly how she planned to pay him back for laughing at her. She could hardly wait to get him alone behind their bedroom door. Smiling wickedly and feeling bold, she allowed her hand to creep up his thick, muscled thigh, right to the apex of his hip-hugging sweat pants. Sam carried her wandering hand to his lips, where he kissed it.

"Explain your opinions about male-female relationships versus female-female relationships," he urged her.

"For starters," she began, "the women friends I have are all able to talk in detail about their feelings. Mary Lou and I decided men tend to lean on the physical side, a habit that can make it tough for them to have a heart-to-heart conversation."

Sam was bothered at her implication they were not as close a couple as women friends could be between themselves. More solemn now than playful, he stared intently at her, his eyes dark as coal. "Are you saying we don't have heart-to-heart talks?"

Bailey pinned him with a silent scrutiny that let him know she was serious. "I'm saying that when the melon gets down to the rind, wouldn't you rather make love to me first and talk to me later?"

Bailey had Sam boxed, cornered, and he knew it. "Right now I'd rather make love," he admitted, "but there's many a time when I'd prefer to hold you while we talk. I've learned sex is better between us when we get the words out of the way."

Bailey blew him a kiss. "Sweet-talk will get you everywhere."

"Good." Dousing the kitchen lights, Sam led her to the couch in the den, where he focused on her lovely and long curling lashes. She snuggled up close, so close he smelled the wonderful scent of her, a fragrance he felt he could find in a storm with his eyes closed if he had to find her that way. Nibbling his bottom lip, he was admirably calm in spite of the sensual fire growing within him.

Bailey glanced at Sam's full bottom lip, the one he

nibbled during deep thought, a sexual distraction for her. What she didn't know was that he nibbled his bottom lip on purpose, subtle payback for the hand she kept on his thigh. He knew she loved to watch him work his lip—so he worked it.

Bailey wiggled in her seat at the sight. "Lita's source says she saw Mary Lou with her lover the week before she died. No one said if Hurley knew about it." Safe within the comfort of Sam's arms, she tried to pretend briefly that scarlet secrets like the one behind Mary Lou's death did not exist. She tried to pretend that life was simple and familiar again, as it had been the last Friday she shared coffee and doughnuts with Mary Lou. Only Bailey could not pretend; there was something dreadfully wrong in the way Mary Lou died—and why.

Sam frowned. "How credible was Lita's source?"

"Very."

"What does your gut feeling tell you?" he asked, as he cast a considering eye across Bailey's face.

"My instinct tells me there's a connection to Mary Lou's affair and her death. I have to find out what happened.

A flicker of apprehension jostled its way to the front of Sam's mind. "You feel betrayed," he stated rather than asked, knowing Bailey the way he did.

"I do. What if Hurley knew about Mary Lou's affair? That would be reason enough for despair."

Sam nodded his head. "True. But at this point I'm not sure it'll do anyone any good to stir things up about Mary Lou. If she cheated on Hurley, it's all over now."

Bailey didn't think so. "It's not over until we know the truth."

Quiet wariness rippled through Sam. "You sound like you're planning something. What?"

"I plan to make the truth my business," she answered quietly. "Good or bad, I want to understand what happened to Mary Lou . . . for Cambria's sake."

"Maybe some things should be left alone, Bailey. I'd think you'd want your memories of Mary Lou to remain joyful. So would Cambria. Think of what trouble you may be stirring."

"Sam, the way things are now, our memories of Mary Lou will be confused and unpleasant," Bailey argued. "At least when Cambria's older, she'll have the chance to know the real reasons behind her mother's death."

"If there were a way to find the truth, I believe you could do it." Sam's eyes warmed with approval.

"Thanks," she returned, her voice sincere. "I'm glad you aren't telling me to mind my own business right now. I crave the truth the way some people crave food."

"And I crave you the way I crave your meals."

Bailey's right eyebrow rose a fraction. "More sweet-talk?" she teased.

"A little," he admitted, half serious. "Honey, we're good together. I can't imagine my life without you. Fern reminds me how blessed I am to have a family."

Bailey turned wistful. "I look forward to our next child."

Sam kissed the tip of her nose. "So do I. Maybe we'll have a daughter with eyes like yours."

She squeezed his thigh. "Or maybe we'll have a son who looks like you." Thoughtful, she ran the warm tips of her fingers along the firm lines of his face,

likening him to a powerful Egyptian pharaoh. Her
heart turned over at the love in his eyes. She rose from
the couch, taking his hand with her. "Let's make our
baby."

Within the security of their bedroom, Sam watched
Bailey's graceful movements as one by one she removed her loafers, jeans, cotton top, satin panties, and
matching bra. The sight of her naked brown body shot
a spear of sweet longing through his groin. In turn, he
disrobed before her, from the T-shirt, sweat pants, and
briefs, to his naked black skin.

The desire Bailey felt as she watched Sam radiated
across her body, leaving her sensually exposed, bare
as water-cleansed stone upon flooded green earth.
When he took her into his arms the luscious sigh she
released was a prelude to the awakening inside her
soul. The sumptuous feeling made her aware in an
earthy way that she and Sam were thigh to thigh, belly
to belly, chest to chest.

She slipped her hand around the nape of his neck,
pulling his lips firmly down toward hers. His mouth
opened to her in an exploration of her unique softness.
In turn, he explored the contours of her face with his
lips, leaving his touch against her cheekbones, her ears,
her brows, her eyelids, and downward across her nose
until he found her mouth again. He kissed her long.
He kissed her good, as carefully, tenderly, they co-
cooned themselves within feelings each aroused in the
other.

Sam could feel Bailey's heart pounding against his
chest, a sensation he understood because his heart beat

the same way. His mouth again took possession of hers, his tongue darting inside like a marauding invader, eager for new conquests. She felt so good to him that when she stroked her fingers across his chest, he reveled in the sensation.

As he fondled her body, she wanted the moment to go on forever until she had tasted, explored, and conquered him one more time. Once again she experienced the wonder of his person, his tall and commanding being whose very existence gave distinct meaning to her life. She moved her hand from behind his waist, lightly stroking his skin from his hips to his chest where she paused to tease one chocolate-tipped nipple.

"You're beautiful," he crooned huskily before he blazed a series of kisses upon her face, her eyes, her brows, her nose, her cheeks, and her eyes. Then carefully, slowly, he covered her mouth. "Touch me," he whispered—and she did, rejoicing in her freedom to explore him in the many ways she had done in their marriage bed. His breath was ragged, a sound that encouraged more lavish exploration. He eased her onto their canopied bed.

"I could look at you all night," she told him.

"Naked?" he asked playfully.

"Totally."

Softly, she moved against him with her hips. Her hands roamed relentlessly across his back then over his chest as though she could not make up her mind where to linger. "I'm ready," she sighed, signaling her decision to give herself to him in a way that reached deeper than the mere parting of her legs. With her words she allowed him entry into her soul, into a place no other man ever delved. She cherished the moment. She cherished him.

Sam eased a slow finger from her body, an act that elicited a lingering groan from Bailey as she lifted her hips to follow him. He watched her face, the little frown between her brows, the hint of perspiration across her forehead, the way her tongue touched her lips, as though tasting him, tasting them together. When he moved to rest between her thighs, she welcomed him, pleased to share her body and soul with the man she loved.

Breakfast for One

Grits
Pan-fried Ham
Scrambled Eggs with
Cheddar Cheese
7-Up over Ice

Six

It was Monday morning. Bailey set about making breakfast for herself after she dropped Fern and Jordanna off at school. Jordanna's mother job-shared at New Generation three days a week as a financial analyst. On those days Bailey took charge of Jordanna, much to Fern's delight.

For breakfast Bailey boiled water for grits which she seasoned with sugar and butter. While the grits thickened she fried an inch-thick slice of smoked ham, a down-home smell she savored because it reminded her of her grandmother's cooking. While the ham sizzled and popped in a cast iron skillet, she scrambled two medium-sized eggs which she flavored with salt, pepper, and cheddar cheese. To wash it all down she poured a glass of 7-Up over several cubes of ice which she topped with a lemon wedge.

Sam always teased Bailey about the size of her breakfast. She ate a lot knowing she would run around all day, burning off the calories. When he gave her a hard time about the cholesterol, she told him the same thing her grandmother always said: "Even though you're hearty and strong, you ain't gonna live forever." Like her grandmother, Bailey ate what she pleased.

During breakfast she was consumed with thoughts

of Mary Lou, her grief entering a new stage, in which her image of Mary Lou emerged as one composed of light wrapped in darkness. Bailey wanted to banish the darkness that now shrouded her friend's memory by finding the truth. She wondered if her search for the truth would reveal whether Mary Lou had been a secret woman with a teasing hint of lightness. Or a light-hearted woman with a seductive darkness, a darkness that ended in death. She meant to find out.

After breakfast she removed the apron covering her jeans and peach-colored sweatshirt, then placed a notepad and pen on the nook table. Thumbing through her private address book, she found Mary Lou's mother's number. Punching in the appropriate digits on her portable phone she held her breath until someone answered the line. She was more nervous than she had ever been in her life.

"Hello," a deep-throated female voice greeted her.

Bailey cleared her own throat as she tried to still the nervous flutters in her stomach. "This is Bailey Walker. I'm calling to speak with Mrs. Perkins if she's available."

Seconds ticked by before the voice chose to respond. When it did, it was cautious. "I'm Yolanda Perkins. How can I help you?"

Uncomfortable about prying into Mrs. Perkins's privacy, yet determined to get to the truth about Mary Lou, Bailey plowed onward, her heart in her throat. "I'm a friend of Mary Lou's, Mrs. Perkins. She gave me your number to call if there was ever an emergency with Cambria while she was away from home painting on a job site."

"I remember you from the funeral and reception.

Mary Lou spoke highly of you and your cooking. The meal you catered was excellent. What can I do for you, Mrs. Walker?" She sounded warm, friendly, sincere.

Bailey steadied her nerves. "The reason I'm calling you is you're probably the only other person who'd understand where I'm coming from right now. I knew Mary Lou for several years. In that time I believe I came to a fair understanding of her personality type, a type that doesn't fit with suicide."

"Go on," Mrs. Perkins prodded.

Patting herself on the back for risking the telephone being slammed in her ear for prying, Bailey warmed to the true topic of her call. "I don't believe Mary Lou jumped to her death," she was surprised at herself for saying. She hadn't even confessed that theory to Sam.

A brief pause. "That's a serious charge, considering Hurley was the witness."

"Yes."

Another brief pause. "Why do you feel this way?"

Bailey expelled a long breath before proceeding. "She wasn't cowardly, or miserable, or unstable. She was devoted to Cambria. Her career was a success. None of her traits added up to suicide."

Mrs. Perkins's voice was strong, powered by a mother's love. "I believe only a bitter woman, a woman who thought she had nothing to give or to receive in the way of love would kill herself. Mary Lou was never such a woman. It's the reason I don't believe she jumped either."

On her notepad Bailey registered Mrs. Perkins's confirmation she did not believe the suicide. Although intangible evidence, the woman's views supported Bailey's estimate of Mary Lou's state of mind at the time of her death—healthy. "Did you tell anyone else your theory?"

Mrs. Perkins laughed, a hollow sound. "Of course I told the rest of our family about my theory but nobody believes me. They consider my judgment impaired with grief."

Bailey took a deep breath, let it out in a rush, and plunged ahead with the question that had nagged her all through breakfast. "Do you think Hurley murdered Mary Lou?" she nearly whispered, appalled by the image.

"Murdered!" Mrs. Perkins sputtered. "He's so cold-hearted, but . . . Hurley . . . Mrs. Walker, I loved my daughter. If there's foul play . . . well, I want the truth, even if it hurts."

Bailey agreed. "I intend to find out exactly why Mary Lou died."

"I can't believe this conversation, but I'm with you." Determination suddenly filled Mrs. Perkins's voice. "How can I help?"

Bailey nibbled the tip of her pen. "Did Mary Lou keep important papers or anything else of significance at your house?"

The reply was crisp. "No. She didn't keep anything here of any value. In the garage there are several boxes of her childhood belongings, nothing she's been into in recent years. And by the way, since we're partners in the solution of this . . . mystery, it's best you call me Yolanda."

Bailey smiled, an action which came across in her voice. "It's a pleasure, Yolanda. Please call me Bailey. I feel better having my hunch backed by you. The fact we both arrived at the same opinion, horrible as it is, gives our theory additional weight."

Yolanda spoke fervently. "I'm so glad Mary Lou had a friend like you."

Bailey blushed, thankful she'd found a comrade in Yolanda Perkins. She'd been feeling like Jane Marple in the Agatha Christie stories, a woman who used her instincts to discover the truth about an incident that didn't *feel* quite right. "You might not think me such a friend when I tell you Mary Lou may have been cheating on Hurley. I think it may be a reason why she died."

Yolanda's voice was mildly surprised. "While I don't condone an affair, mind you, if Mary Lou was sidetracked, well—she told me she found out Hurley was seeing some woman he worked with."

This time Bailey paused. When she spoke, she sounded subdued, thoughtful. How long had Hurley cheated on Mary Lou? And she on him? "I thought you said Hurley was cold?"

"Even cold men have appetites," Yolanda explained. "You see, Hurley wasn't the man he seemed. Hurley was critical of Mary Lou's work even though he bragged about it with his physician friends and at family gatherings. In private he gave her a hard time."

Bailey frowned, unaware of the facade. "Mary Lou never spoke of it."

Yolanda sighed. "My daughter is . . . was a proud woman. She wouldn't admit she had trouble with Hurley. I found out because I overheard him criticizing her about her art one evening when he thought no one was listening."

Baffled, Bailey remembered most of Mary Lou's referrals stemmed from her husband. "Why did he give Mary Lou a hard time about her work?"

Yolanda spoke with quiet emphasis. "Hurley is a man with no substance. He's one of those men who hates it when his wife outshines him, even for thirty seconds. He's a bigshot physician, a good-looking man accustomed to having his own way. He married Mary Lou because she was smart, attractive, talented, and a homebody. She suited his prospering image as much as his silk ties and solid-gold cuff links."

The scorn in Yolanda's voice did not escape Bailey. "You don't care too much for Hurley," she observed.

Yolanda sniffed disdainfully. "I did in the beginning of their marriage, but Hurley changed. He both envied and despised Mary Lou's talent. When one of his physician buddies saw the way she had painted the inside of their home, he commissioned her to paint a mural in his reception room, a design featuring an ocean theme, Mary Lou's specialty. After that offers came in regularly. Hurley went along with it, even though he didn't like it."

"Why did Mary Lou marry him if he's as spiteful and cold-hearted as you say he is?"

Yolanda released a mirthless chuckle. "Oh, Hurley could lay on the charm when it suited him. He treated Mary Lou like a queen when they courted, then later when in public. She wanted to build a solid future with someone as strong and ambitious as her father, president and founder of the African American Boys Club in New Hope. Mary Lou's mistake was to pick a man with loads of ambition and too little heart."

Intrigued by this revelation into Mary Lou's character, Bailey pressed the telephone closer to her ear as she sought more information. She now knew Mary Lou and Hurley had marital problems. "Do you think Mary Lou may have cheated on Hurley out of revenge because he cheated on her first?"

"I don't like thinking that way about my only daughter. But Mary Lou was a passionate woman, surely you know that." Bailey kept quiet as she noted this characteristic to herself.

"If she was angry with Hurley for breaking fidelity vows," Yolanda continued, "I can imagine her seeking revenge. What do you plan to do next?"

Bailey flipped a page backward in her notepad. "First find out where Hurley took Cambria. Second, find the name of the man Mary Lou was involved with."

Yolanda paused. "But Cambria lives with me."

Bailey gasped, shocked. "What!"

Yolanda expressed her concerns. "Hurley said it would be best if Cambria was out of the house, away from the memories. Until you called, I was busy convincing myself he didn't want Cambria because he was throwing himself into his work as a way to grieve Mary Lou's death. Now I'm not sure about his reasons. I'm glad to have Cambria with me, where she's safe."

So was Bailey. "Where did he move?"

"Flamingo Hill."

Bailey wrote the address on her notepad. She was surprised to know Hurley had moved to the upper-class neighborhood, an area where nothing quaint or old-fashioned existed as it did on Daisy Lane. Flamingo Hill was one of New Hope Township's most elegant, upscale residential districts.

"How is Cambria?" she asked, remembering how

fragile the child had appeared at the funeral and reception.

"She's talking about her feelings. My husband and I believe it's a good sign."

"I'm glad she has you, Yolanda."

"Always. We attend grief counseling together in order to deal with our loss. I assure you, Bailey, Cambria won't be without love or support as she matures into a lovely woman. I'm young enough to continue where my daughter left off. Oh, Bailey," Yolanda started slowly, "why didn't you come to my home with your theory about Mary Lou?"

Bailey's voice held a tinge of discomfort. "I thought the distance might help us both. I didn't know how you'd react to my suspicions. If you were angry, you'd be free to slam the phone in my ear, something I'd prefer over a slap to the face."

"I understand, considering the nature of this call. Promise me though that next time you'll come on over. You've given me hope. I can't stand thinking Mary Lou killed herself."

Warmth spread through Bailey. "Promise."

"Keep me posted."

"I will."

"And Bailey . . . thank you."

After putting Fern to bed, Bailey sat with Sam in the kitchen at the nook table, telling him about her day. She began with her conversation with Yolanda, ending with her desire to find Mary Lou's private papers for a solid clue—maybe even the identity of the other man in her life. "Plus," Bailey added, "I have a suspicion that Hurley is more involved in Mary Lou's death than he's let on."

"What do you think, that he murdered her?" Sam said with a chuckle.

"Yes, I do."

Sam's eyes widened with surprise. "Hurley Booker killed his wife? You conclude *that* from your conversation today?"

"Not just today but ever since her death. You know I've always thought that the way she died made no sense. Now, that I've found out about Mary Lou's affair, Hurley's infidelity, and the details of Mary Lou's marriage—the pieces are coming together."

"What pieces?" Sam's concern for Bailey's safety showed in his voice. "Hurley is a respected doctor. Yolanda is a grieving mother. An unaffectionate man whose wife is cheating on him isn't necessarily a suspect for murder."

"In this case, to me, he is."

Looking fit in navy cotton gym shorts and an indigo-colored cropped top, Sam decided to switch tactics. "Assuming you could gain access to Mary Lou's private things, what would you search for?"

"Anything strange. Even though Mary Lou was a wizard at artistry, she was rotten at filing papers. She told me she tossed new mail and paid bills in brown paper bags until ready to file them on a rainy day."

Sam puzzled over this bit of news. "Hurley may have thrown them away. Or simply filed them."

Bailey shrugged. "He left in such a hurry, I doubt he did much more than toss stuff in boxes."

His gentle nature at odds with his powerful build,

Sam walked up to Bailey in order to massage her tension-filled back and shoulders. "Now what?"

Bailey leaned into her husband's strong chest, welcoming the comfort he provided in generous measure. Glad to be of service, Sam kissed the top of her head, his ministrations almost sidetracking her.

"I'm going to Flamingo Hill," she answered, her voice velvet over steel.

Sam stiffened. "I'm going with you. If you're right and Hurley's guilty of murder, he's a dangerous man. We'll do this together."

It was Tuesday morning. Bailey did not have much to say during the winding drive to the redwood-studded Flamingo Hill. She was too caught up in her thoughts. What if she were wrong? she wondered. What if she simply did not know Mary Lou well enough to tell if she were suicidal? After all, she didn't know she may have been having an affair. But something told her she was absolutely right.

It took ten minutes to find Hurley's hefty-sized house once they reached the area. Secluded in a nest of towering maples and oaks, Mary Lou's husband had secured a small mansion.

Surprised at Hurley's new lodgings, Sam said, "Big jump for short notice, wouldn't you say?"

Wearing jeans and a red blouse, Bailey whistled appreciatively. "I'll say it's a big jump. The land alone must cost more than their house on Daisy Lane."

Flamingo Hill was a prestigious settlement, a standout jewel among a city of emerald-colored trees. Bailey likened the development to a true flamingo.

Like its namesake, Hurley's new neighborhood preened in homes painted in pink to crimson splendor. With its color-coordinated homes, its lush lawns, and private roads, the area was the perfect place for a prominent man to assume a circumspect lifestyle. It was obvious to Bailey that Hurley's move had been well planned. This hinted to her that if Hurley murdered Mary Lou, it had not been during a heated moment.

Dressed in stone-washed denims and a green shirt, Sam looked at his watch. "We'd best get busy. When we called, no one was home. That could change."

"Let's try the doors and windows," Bailey suggested as they picked their way between the clipped privet hedges lining the narrow sidewalk. The walkway led to the wide front door, a door as solid and imposing as the mansion itself. At the base of the front steps sat a two-foot-high stone tortoise folly. The yard ornament peered out from a purple alyssum border.

While the amateur sleuths checked for entry into Hurley's home, absolute zero activity went on around the Booker property. No birds chirped in cheerful play. No bees hummed between end-of-spring flowers. Without Mary Lou's vibrant touch, Hurley's new home lacked an inviting appeal. Instead, it looked imposing and cold, like its owner.

Suddenly fully aware of Mary Lou's influence upon her immediate world, Sam marveled at the difference one human being could make, a difference involving subtle yet exquisite beauty, a beauty evident in the family's private domain. He was glad Bailey was not hunting alone for clues in the austere setting of Flamingo Hill. He linked his fingers with hers, unaware of the sense of security that seeped into her at the contact, a contact that reinforced their mutual love and respect.

They went to the front door. No one answered. They went to the garage. It was locked, as were the first floor windows. Bailey was deeply disappointed. "Well, this is a bust."

"It was a long shot to begin with."

"Sam?"

"Yes?"

"How did you feel about snooping?"

"Same as you. Scared. Excited."

"Too scared to do it again?"

He glanced at his wristwatch, noting there were three hours left until they needed to pick Fern up from school. "What do you have in mind?"

"The Bookers' old house. Maybe Mary Lou's things are still there."

"Let's find out."

Sitting in their burgundy minivan, Sam and Bailey regrouped. They were down the street from Mary Lou's house in the New Hope Community Center parking lot. They parked there in order to better blend their car with the neighborhood. Parking in front of Mary Lou's vacant house was too conspicuous.

Anxiety pumped through Bailey's body as she contemplated her next adventure with Sam. "It would've been easier to break into Hurley's house on Flamingo Hill. There was less commotion."

Sensing her anxiety, Sam sought to reassure her. "Actually, we're better off here. This neighborhood is active because of the community center. At this moment the lot has several minivans in it, two of them Previas."

"I hadn't thought of it that way. I guess I'm just nervous." She reached for his hand. "I'm glad you're here."

"We'll be fine. It isn't likely Hurley will show up. If a real estate person comes around we'll leave phony names and claim we're prospective house buyers."

Bailey cast a quizzical look at Sam. "You're really getting into this, aren't you?"

"Yes," he admitted, with a smile. "The more I hear about Mary Lou, the more I agree with you that something strange is going on. If you're going snooping, I don't want you to be alone."

Bailey looked outside the passenger window. "I feel like the whole world is watching us cross the line between Good Samaritans and bumbling crooks."

"As long as we act like we have every reason to be in the area people won't consider us strange. Act normal."

Bringing her nerves under control, Bailey heaved a huge breath into her lungs, let it out slowly, then advanced from the minivan. She slung her leather purse over her left shoulder as she walked briskly around the front of the car to stand beside Sam.

Hand in hand they walked the short distance to Mary Lou's house. The plantation-style home looked the same as it always did—classic. The pale pink flowering dogwood trees that lined the walk to Mary Lou's front door were in excellent form.

Bailey tipped her face upward in order to look into Sam's attentive eyes. "Mary Lou kept a spare key in the backyard gazebo. Hurley may have left it by mistake."

"Let's check."

Sam was tall enough to lift the latch on the side yard gate with ease. Ushering Bailey inside, he shut the gate quickly with an economy of noise. Still, he listened for the sound of a curious neighbor. He hadn't seen anyone watching them walk to the gate, but he wanted to be careful.

Walking across the backyard, Bailey tried to remember exactly where Mary Lou once said she kept her spare key. She had told Bailey about the key during one of their Friday morning get-togethers. Their topic at the time had been how they managed to get back into their home after they were locked out by mistake. Remembering where the key was kept, Bailey went to her knees. On her knees, she peered into a dirt-splattered slot, an action that brought her face-to-face with a large gray spider. After blowing on the insect until it scurried away she slipped her index finger into the narrow slot and was rewarded with the cold metal feel of Mary Lou's emergency house key. She grinned at Sam, "So far, so good."

Buoyed by their stroke of good luck, Sam grinned back. "Let's hope Hurley hasn't changed the lock on the kitchen door." He hadn't.

With double-agent stealth, Sam and Bailey entered Mary Lou's house, taking care to lock the door again behind them.

"The inside of this place still sparkles," Sam acknowledged, noticing how clean the floors, counters, and walls remained even after Hurley's hasty move. In his mind's eye he remembered how the home had been filled with living floral arrangements. The house now smelled stale.

The still air inside the vacant house created a powerful urge in Bailey to crack the miniblind-covered windows. They did not open the windows because doing so might flag an alert neighbor to the fact the supposedly empty house was no longer empty.

More curious than ever about Mary Lou, Sam was as eager as Bailey to discover what Hurley had left behind, if anything. "Let's split up. You search the house while I check the garage and attic."

"Deal."

Bailey cruised quickly through the house. Without its fine, tasteful furniture and assorted bric-a-brac, Mary Lou's house was devoid of personality but not devoid of presence. Her presence bounced against denuded walls everywhere. Looking at the switch-plates Bailey noticed the beautiful murals.

Each tiny mural was distinctive. In Cambria's bedroom there were ponds with graceful swans. Dancing teddy bears leapt about with umbrellas in the rain. Pretty pigs exercised in pool water. Bailey walked through the house, examining more closely than she ever had the various themes of the switch-plate murals. She noticed that only in the kitchen did the switch-plate cover not blend into the wall. It stood out. Instead of being a shade of blue or green, it was a pale peach matching the ocean life. In every other room the plate cover matched the water. "Hmm," Bailey murmured. "Interesting."

When Sam returned from the garage and attic empty-handed, he found Bailey opening the switch-plate cover with a nail file from her purse.

"What are you doing?" he asked.

"This plate doesn't belong here," she said, returning her attention to the switch-plate. She used the metal nail file to unfasten the screws that held the cover in place. She removed the cover. Taped to its back with wide transparent tape was a tiny metal key. Excitement shot through Bailey at the find.

"This is weird," Sam decided. Cautiously, he ran his fingers around the inner edges of the rectangular shaped hole behind the cover to assure himself there were no other surprises. Finding nothing, he replaced the cover. "We should check all the others."

"Good idea." Bailey handed him her nail clippers so he could use its miniature file.

Room by room they searched the house, finding nothing more that was unusual. When they returned the last screw to its proper place, Sam glanced at his wristwatch. "Fern's school lets out in fifteen minutes. Time to go."

Linking her arm with Sam and grinning like crazy, Bailey agreed. "Ready, partner."

Romantic Respite
for Two

Strawberry Salad
Oyster Pilaf
Chilled Champagne

Seven

After breaking into two homes, Sam and Bailey needed to unwind. Their brazen acts were packed with more adrenaline than either was used to handling, making an evening at home an important step toward regaining a normal, even keel. Only then would they return their minds to the silver key.

While Sam helped Fern finish her homework, Bailey prepared enough dinner food so that there would be leftovers to eat during the all-night rap session they had in mind. They planned to set their minds straight about where they were headed regarding Mary Lou Booker's demise.

Wearing a Hawaiian print sundress, Bailey started off dinner preparation with oyster pilaf, their talk-all-night dinner favorite. From the well-stocked refrigerator she quickly pulled out celery, scallions, parsley, mushrooms, and oysters. From a cupboard she took out a handy bottle of cooking wine, seasonings, and rice.

In separate plastic mixing bowls she placed the sliced celery, chopped scallions, and sliced mushrooms. Once the vegetables sauteed in butter to her satisfaction she added oysters to the hot pan, cooking them until their edges began to curl. After that she added wine, rice, and parsley, all of which she seasoned to taste.

For the strawberry salad Bailey hand-picked ripe red berries from her garden. These she rinsed and sliced before squeezing tangy lemon juice over the pieces. She filled a metal measuring cup with creamy mayonnaise, and tossed in a handful of walnuts.

Sam and Fern had already made a run to the local supermarket to purchase the presliced and cored pineapple she needed for the salad which she diced into bite-sized pieces. She mixed all her ingredients together before tossing them with ripe green lettuce from her generous garden.

With champagne chilling in the refrigerator, all she had to do was set the redwood table outside the master suite with the elegant dishes her sister, Daphne, had given them as a wedding present. The gold-trimmed ivory china, sterling silver cutlery, and elegant champagne flutes adorned the periwinkle linen tablecloth. Vanilla-scented ivory candles provided the ambiance.

Once Fern had been read to and put to bed after the family dinner, Sam and Bailey closed their bedroom door for solace and relaxation. With the house quiet, Sam lifted Bailey into his arms for a soulful kiss. When he put her down she rose on tiptoe so she could kiss him again.

Growing more aroused by every passing second, Sam ticked off the stunning particulars regarding his wife. Her graceful movements were a pleasure to watch, a sensuous pleasure that shot a spear of sweet longing through his body.

In her own turn, Bailey collided eyes with the most gorgeous man she had ever known. The desire she felt upon visual contact radiated across her senses, leaving her riveted with attraction. After their adventures of the day she was more sexually charged than she had been in her life. Transfixed, her wide eyes locked in primal communion with the man who had snatched her breath clean away at first sight.

When Sam's gaze met with Bailey's, her spirits soared with desire. The long sigh she emitted showed she anticipated the delicious unveiling of their physical rapture. Her pulse quickened. Somewhat breathless, she advanced closer to the only man who had ever had the power to ring her sexual bell this hard. Sam's unique sexual bell-ringing ability delighted her because it made her feel spectacular to be alive and all woman.

Looking at her husband in the privacy of their bedroom, Bailey considered the concepts of destiny and fate, concepts she had viewed as distinct until clicking thick lashes with Sam for the first time. Until then she had merely viewed these concepts as interchangeable. After deepening her initial acquaintance with Sam she realized she had been wrong because destiny, an inevitable course of events was not equal to its cousin, fate.

Fate, a force of supernatural will could be influenced by chance. Certain as she was that night followed day, Bailey believed her union with Sam was her ultimate destiny, a destiny that could not be altered by chance, by will, or by reason. She belonged to him, and he to her.

To Bailey's greedy eyes Sam looked as tasty as an orange Popsicle on a sweltering hot day, so tasty her mouth watered at the delicious sweet sight of him.

With his long ebony body, wide shoulders, and thick but nimble neck, Sam Walker was loaded with sexual power. Like an electric billboard, neon words flashed with bright clarity into Bailey's mind, neon words like *intense, profound,* and *exciting.* In the heartbeats since he had shut the bedroom door behind him, creating a silent, sensual world for two, Bailey was rocked with an unprecedented vision of herself being tantalized to screaming point by the hot, moist tip of his tongue in the most treasured places of her body.

Deeply aroused himself, Sam cozied right up to her without saying a word as he took in the essence pulsing from her body's most sexual core. It radiated outward, ensnaring him within her feminine net. She was so close to him, he saw the fine lines beside her thick lower lashes, lashes he touched with the tips of his sensitized fingers. "You're like water to a thirsty man," he exalted, his rich voice running between them smooth and hot like lavish, bold-tasting liquid.

"Drink me dry," she purred, her skin warmed by the voluptuous allure that rippled like water around them.

Taking her silken elbow into the solid grasp of his fingers, Sam led her to a cozy set of chairs near an elongated picture window in order to sip champagne. The stuffed chairs were set on either side of an occasional table. While Bailey draped one shapely leg across the other, she noticed the consummate interest in which Sam studied her thighs. When his roving eyes flickered with lust, she knew he had spotted again the large round mole on her right knee. When he licked his lips as if he wanted to taste the spot, she smiled at his gesture, thrilled by the carnal thoughts she could see in his eyes.

"Tease," he claimed indulgently.

A wicked thrill shot through Bailey at his words. "Don't I please you, too?"

"Always." His eyes sharp and assessing, Sam slid his fingers down the padded arm of his chair. In his mind he imagined it was Bailey's arm he touched instead of the chair's, a thought that fueled a thickening in his groin.

"When you look at me like this I feel on top of the world," she confided as she peered at him seductively. In truth, he took her to the top of the world and beyond. A low, deep, and languid sound flowed from Sam's lips at her compliment. The luxuriant cadence enchanted Bailey, enthralled her sensual self so much, she leaned forward in her seat to take advantage of every nerve-tingling nuance. She marveled at his sexy laughter, the way it made her feel warm and desired as if she were the only woman in the world he would ever spend this kind of time with.

Lifting his champagne flute, Sam toasted his wife. Placing his open palm across the heart side of his chest, Sam celebrated their loving communion with a kiss. His kiss seared Bailey until her toes flexed and curled in sexual tension. She groaned. At the sound, Sam increased the pleasing pressure of his lips, the expert within himself stoking her fire until they were both consumed. When his lips scorched up and down her neck, she shivered. As his tongue progressed to the lobes of her ears, she sighed, a sound so sweet it quickened his pulse. Sam groaned.

Pressed as close as she was to his chest, Bailey felt as well as heard his groan. It electrified her mind to know she could make a powerful man do that with just a kiss. Enraptured, she stripped her sundress off her shoulders, flinging it to the carpeted floor, her body infused with a woman's ultimate power—the power to heal, to nourish, and to renew; even if that power was used to heal, to nourish, and to renew only one man, one integral aspect of the universe.

Mesmerized, Sam watched as Bailey shed her colorful clothing, attire that fell from her body in a soft heap on the floor. Breathing hard, he responded in kind. Off went his cotton walking shorts. Off went the matching olive shirt. He understood her as completely as she understood him. They wanted it all.

Mind.

Body.

Soul.

Leaning forward, Bailey shivered with uncontrollable quakes which let Sam know she, too, was thirsty; she, too, was hungry, eager for physical love. Her luscious lips half parted, she sucked up every heady sensation of Sam she could absorb. In the airtight space of their intimate, all-consuming world, he was everything Bailey wanted in that sliver of time.

Hard.

Solid.

Man.

In this suspended, sacred world of their own making, Bailey cared for nothing except the way her husband made her feel—luscious, rare, and carnal. Her pulse danced with pleasure when she filled her hands with his biceps. They were big and hard in her hands. In slow motion she watched his mouth descend once more from its scintillating height to rest firmly against her own mouth. She pressed herself against him, so close she felt the hard length at the apex of his thighs. It was a hardness she welcomed because it carried the seed of life.

Sam tumbled in their sexual heaven, a heaven filled with psychedelic stars and all because she was kissing him the way she wanted to kiss him, as if he held the key to the gates of eternity. She kissed him as if he were the only man alive, the only man she wanted to spend the last ten seconds on earth with. He reveled in being her private treasure, taboo to every woman created except her. Enthralled, he took every kiss she gave him, giving her more in return. Their prolonged desire urged him to make love with Bailey, deep love, serious love, long and tender love.

Lifting her, he sheltered her inside his arms, fluidly maneuvering himself to the table beside the chair she had vacated brief sexy moments before. He brought himself to the table's edge and positioned her to stand between his thighs where he scattered salsa-hot kisses across her champion cheekbones, beautiful brows, and faultless forehead. He kissed her tender temples, charming chin, then lustrous lips once again. When he finished, he didn't know where he ended and she began.

Passion-drunk, Sam hooked three fingers underneath Bailey's chin then lifted her face in order to read her expression more clearly. What he saw erased the past from his mind then turned around and erased the present. What he saw made him think about the future, a future spent growing old together. It was thinking of the future that fired his spirit so much that when Sam spoke to Bailey again, his voice was strong, deep, and throaty, as strong and as deeply unforgettable as the man himself. "Ready?"

"Yes." Sam's body looked good to Bailey. She liked his six-foot build, his ebony skin, his wavy hair, his jet-black eyes, thick brows, broad nose, and sensuous, strong dark lips. It was Sam's thoroughly kissable lips that set her blood boiling. He was a loyal, loving man with his warm-hearted woman, a complementary young couple serenaded with Marvin Gaye classics crooning in the sensuous, scintillating background.

Eager for sexual healing, Sam lifted his willing wife into his arms. He carried her with powerful strides to their fragrant bed. Along the way, he experienced the thrill of her fingers against his beautiful back. He enjoyed their touch along his contoured shoulders as she clung, like apple-scented geranium to his muscular length.

The melting magic of Sam's tongue against Bailey's mouth, his lips against her pulses pushed away thoughts of Mary Lou's death and the Booker family tragedy. "Sam," she said breathlessly, "You're making me crazy."

He grinned slowly. "Only to sweeten our pleasure."

"Everything you do feels good," she admitted, trailing the line of his chin with the softest of bites.

The ardor in Sam's eyes shone as bright as the twin flames burning slowly on their intimate table for two. With infinite care he pressed her body more firmly against him, reveling in the feel of her nipples as they grazed the dark hairs scattered across his chest. When at last their bodies melded as one, there was no uncertain tomorrow, no fleeting yesterday. They were safe within the sanctuary of their spacious canopied bed, a bed filled to flowing with plump pillows and soft linen.

Within this private haven, they surrendered each to the other—their pride, their devotion, their enduring love.

After bathing, they swathed themselves in matching terrycloth robes. Naked beneath the navy fabric, they carried trays of hot food to their table for two. It was now time to get down to the business of love within a marriage, the honest commitment to stand by each other through thick and thin.

"For starters, I don't want you to endanger yourself by snooping into Mary Lou's affairs on your own. I've got to be with you. Okay?" Sam said.

"Okay."

Sam took a bite of strawberry salad. "I'm amazed you found the hidden switch-plate key. Your intuitive skills impress me. I bet not one man in a thousand would have been as observant and clever as you, Sherlock."

Bailey speared a berry from Sam's salad. "I'm glad I'm not one man in a thousand, Watson."

Sam grinned, recalling their recent sex. "So am I." Putting down his fork, he toyed with her fingers, thinking she had lovely hands, healing hands, soul-food-cooking hands. "Tomorrow I'm arranging a leave of absence," he announced solemnly. "I can't let you do this alone—and I know you won't put this puzzle aside until it's solved," he said with an uneasy laugh. "Plus I can't shake the feeling there's a time bomb ticking away regarding Mary Lou's death."

Bailey was relieved and surprised by Sam's gesture. "Can you honestly get away from the office under such short notice?"

Sam shrugged. "I simply need to delegate the work flow to several competent senior engineers. Things will be fine."

Bailey squeezed his hand. "Sam?"

"Yes."

"What makes you believe me about Mary Lou not being the kind of person to commit suicide?"

"Besides your strong belief?" he said with a smile. "Her art."

"What do you mean?"

"Her art is peaceful," he explained, thinking his way through as he spoke aloud. "Her home was well kept and peaceful. The few times I'd spoken with her she was warm and charming. While we didn't know about her possibly having an affair, her passions seemed to funnel into her art and her care for Cambria—not violence. At the same time, my opinion of Hurley is rapidly changing."

Bailey's eyes widened with interest. "What changed your mind about Hurley?"

Sam frowned. "The way he abandoned Cambria. I could never do that to Fern. I don't believe any loving father would be able to do it either. I'd like to know more about Hurley. Do you think Minette could shed any light on his character?"

Bailey tapped her right index finger against the tabletop. "I can ask."

"We'll do it together."

"Good idea," Bailey agreed, her tone enthusiastic.

"At the end of the week we'll turn our findings in to the police," Sam admitted as he lifted Bailey's hands from the table to place them between his own. Once Mary Lou's hands had been as warm, as soft, and as talented as Bailey's. A sense of horror touched him as he squeezed Bailey's hands even tighter and wondered if all their snooping might lead them into trouble.

Teatime for the Blues

Buttermilk Scones
Strawberry Jam
Cinnamon-Orange Herbal Tea

Eight

It was Thursday morning. Sam was arranging time off at work. Fern was at school. Dressed in red shorts and a blue sleeveless sweater, Bailey picked up the cordless telephone in order to call Yolanda Perkins about meeting with her and Sam. When she picked up the receiver, she could not get a dial tone. Puzzled, she pressed the "phone button" to reactivate the line. The phone was dead. She went into the den and picked up the receiver there only to discover this phone was also dead. Closing her eyes, Bailey mentally went through the motions of paying bills, double-checking to remember if she had paid the phone bill on time. She had.

Grumbling softly, she decided to walk two houses down the street to Mrs. MacAllister's in order to call the telephone company. Mrs. MacAllister was a friendly seventy-year-old retired seamstress. As Bailey walked out of the den, she gasped in shock as someone strong threw a dark cloth sack over her head, yanking it tightly around her straining neck. Her scream was cut short when a cold, hard, and blunt object poked hurtfully in the small of her back.

"Where are they?"

Bailey's throat went dry. Her heart thudded against her chest. "What?" she managed to croak.

"The pictures Mary Lou gave you," the voice hissed.

Bailey could scarcely breathe. "She didn't give me anything," she answered hoarsely due to fear and the thick bag around her head.

Frustrated, the intruder snarled savagely then twisted the sack opening tighter around Bailey's neck, an action that made her gag. All she could think about was Fern and Sam, how she might never see them again.

"Don't let what happened to her, happen to you," the menacing voice warned before flinging Bailey hard against a wall. She crumpled in a heap on the floor.

By the time she removed the dark sack from her muzzy head, the intruder had vanished. Shaking, she ran through the front door and down the street to Mrs. MacAllister's yellow house. After one quick look at Bailey's distraught face through her peephole, the gray-haired woman yanked open her front door in a hurry.

"What happened?" Mrs. MacAllister queried, her kind face a wonderful collection of distinctive buckskin-colored wrinkles. Draping her arms around Bailey's shoulders, she surged with maternal instincts. She led Bailey inside. "Tell me what's wrong," she insisted gently.

Bailey did, watching Mrs. MacAllister's eyes widen and narrow at the details of her story. Aghast by what had happened, the elderly woman did not simply want to call the New Hope Township Police Department. She wanted to call someone efficient, someone who could make sure Bailey would stay safe. She called someone specific on the police force, her thirty-two-year-old grandson, Homicide Detective Ridge Williams. Next Bailey called Sam. She also called Jordanna's mother at work about caring for Fern after school if it was necessary. Once she knew she had backup childcare for Fern, Bailey allowed herself to burst into tears.

Leaving Bailey briefly alone to cry stress-relieving tears, Mrs. MacAllister brewed a mug of chamomile tea, her sure-fire cure to soothe ragged nerves. It pleased her to see her young neighbor revive from the warmth of the steaming tea, a liquid that helped steel Bailey for what was ahead of her as she relived the episode when she explained what had happened to the police and Sam. Although she looked forward to telling the police her theory on why she was attacked so they could start an investigation into Mary Lou's death, she was not looking forward to facing Sam. After all, his biggest fear, that someone would attempt to harm her, had materialized.

Strong-looking, dashing, and handsome, Homicide Detective Ridge Williams arrived quickly. He was six-feet-four-inches tall. His milk-chocolate complexion matched the rich shade of his expressive voice. The dimples in his cheeks belied the severity of his beakish nose, as did the ultrawhite glare of his teeth. He wore a charcoal gabardine suit, dress shirt, and geometric patterned silk tie.

After assuring his paternal grandmother she had done the right thing by calling him direct he made certain Bailey did not require medical care. Because she didn't, he escorted her home where he took his time investigating the crime scene. He sought and collected evidence using a field investigation kit. Slowly, carefully, he checked the area for signs of the intruder,

miscellaneous objects the attacker may have left behind, like a button or a piece of jewelry. Other than
the dark sack, he did not find a thing. After his search,
Detective Williams sat down with a still-shaken Bailey
in the kitchen in order to ask her about possible suspects and motive.

"Tell me about your suspicions," the detective re-
quested.

Bailey was glad to tell all she knew to someone
official. "Well, first of all, there's been a mysterious
death."

"Go on," the detective encouraged, his notepad and
mechanical pencil ready.

"My friend, Mary Lou Booker, jumped to her death
over the side of a pleasure cruise ship on the bay recently. It was the eve of her wedding anniversary."

"Had she been depressed?"

"No."

The detective had heard about the suicide on a local
news station. "And you think she was . . . pushed?"

Bailey looked the detective square in the eye. "Yeah.
I guess so."

In his years as a police officer, Detective Williams
had soon learned that there were idiosyncrasies about
victims that only their family and friends would notice.
He considered Bailey's opinion an asset, not a hin-
drance. "Do you have a suspect in mind?"

"Yes."

"Who?"

"Her husband, Hurley. He claims he witnessed Mary
Lou jump."

"And you think Hurley Booker attacked you today?"
The detective's tone was neutral.

"Yes."

"Why?"

"I've got five reasons to think he did it."

The detective flipped his notepad to a fresh page. "Go ahead with item one."

Bailey thought about Hurley letting his daughter cry herself to sleep. "He's a cold man, probably ruthless. He moved into a mansion on Flamingo Hill the day after his wife's funeral. His wife never mentioned to me they were house-hunting."

"Okay," said the detective. "Item two."

Bailey thought about Hurley's height, good health, and body strength. "He had the physical ability to shove her overboard."

"Item three?"

Bailey remembered Hurley was the only witness. "He had opportunity. He and Mary Lou were alone on the portion of the ship where Mary Lou had gone over the side."

Ridge pressed the top of his mechanical pencil to sharpen its point. "Item four?"

"He had a motive which was revenge. She was having an affair. I don't know his name yet."

The detective lifted a brow at the word yet. "And five?" he prompted.

"The person who attacked me today was a man. There are only two men I can think of who might have a reason to hurt Mary Lou. One man was the guy she was having an affair with. The other man was Hurley, and he was the only person to witness her jump ship. Since I've been openly suspicious about her suicide, I'm the logical person Mary Lou's murderer would want to scare off his trail. Detective, I don't think Mary

Lou Booker committed suicide because she loved life, a joy she expressed by the way she cared for her daughter and painted murals."

"If Hurley was going to murder Mary Lou, wouldn't he just push her overboard and say it was an accident?"

"No."

"Why?"

Bailey remembered a conversation she and Mary Lou once shared over Friday morning coffee. They were discussing private phobias. "Mary Lou wouldn't put herself in position to fall overboard by accident. She couldn't swim."

The detective smiled. "I'm impressed, Mrs. Walker. You've given this a lot of thought."

Bailey remembered how close she had come to losing her life that day. She stroked her neck. "I prefer to die of old age, Detective Williams, not murder. Mary Lou's death needs to be examined again by the police. As far as I'm concerned, the question isn't *who* killed Mary Lou, but *why.*"

The detective took a few moments to review his notes with Bailey while she waited for Sam to arrive. At the sound of tires screeching to a halt in the driveway, Bailey announced somewhat breathlessly, "That's my husband."

The detective put away his mechanical pencil and notepad, recognizing Bailey's need for comfort. "I discourage you from any deeper investigation into Mary Lou Booker's death, Mrs. Walker. I'll look into it from here on. I'll contact you within a few days." Giving her his business card, he added, "Call me day or night should you think of anything new or helpful regarding Mary Lou Booker's death or the attack on you today."

"I will," Bailey promised, fear stark and livid in her eyes. She could hardly wait to find comfort in Sam's arms.

Terror-stricken over what he would find, Sam leapt up the front steps and raced through the house until he found her in the kitchen with the detective. Thankful for her safety, he swept her into his arms as if he would never let her go. "Are you okay? Do you need a doctor?" He ran his hands over her arms, turning her around to touch her with his eyes.

"My throat hurts," she croaked, stroking the skin of her neck. "I think it's temporary."

"I'm so glad. After you called, I couldn't get here fast enough."

Turning to the detective, he offered his hand. "Did she tell you about Hurley Booker?"

"Yes." The detective's grip was firm. "I told her not to investigate further."

"Good."

"I'll keep you posted," the detective promised. Turning to Bailey, he said, "In the meantime, please call me day or night should you recall something specific."

Putting his arm around Bailey's shoulders, Sam nodded his head. "Will do."

When the twinkling-eyed detective took his leave, Sam studied the bruise marks on his wife's slim neck. He clenched his fists, hating he had not been there to defend her. "Life has no meaning without you and Fern, Bailey. None."

Bailey cupped her husband's face inside her strong, capable hands. "I believe the intruder wanted to scare me, not hurt me."

Sam ran a tense hand around the nape of his neck,

his nerves on edge with the remnants of fear. "It must be Hurley. If it weren't for Detective Williams, I'd be on my way to question him myself."

"That's what I told him."

Whenever Bailey was bogged down in bone-deep blues as she was on the night of her attack, she baked fragrant buttermilk scones and had them with spicy cinnamon-orange tea. The blues were always chased away by the decadent hot buttered bread dripping with sparkling strawberry jam. Time alone with good-hearted Sam did not completely soothe her jagged emotions. After her ordeal, she needed to reach down deep inside herself for courage and strength, especially since Hurley phoned after the detective left their house to say he planned to stop by the Walkers' later that evening. Sam didn't like the idea but welcomed the chance to get things out in the open.

Her grandmother once told Bailey that sometimes when the bone-deep blues hits a woman, she needs more than a man, more than a sister-girlfriend. Sometimes she needs to be alone, quiet within her own spirit. That was the kind of solitude Bailey created for herself after Fern had been settled down, assured everything would be all right.

Thanks to Sam, Bailey had the kitchen all to herself. Dressed in a garnet sweater with matching stirrup pants, she was methodic, functioning more on automatic than true conscious thought as she secured from the refrigerator the ingredients she needed to make the blues-busting buttermilk scones. She gathered flour, baking powder, sugar, baking soda, salt, butter, egg, vanilla, buttermilk, and sun-dried currants.

In a wide mixing bowl she combined the salt, baking soda, baking powder, sugar, and flour. Into the dry ingredients she dropped dollops of flavor-boosting butter. This she quickly cut into the dry mixture with a pastry cutter. After achieving the desired crumbly texture, she added the vanilla, egg, buttermilk, and currants.

She rolled the scone dough out on a floured board in the same way she rolled out dough for biscuits on Saturday mornings. She flour-dusted her hands, then flattened the buttermilk dough into an even circle on a well-used aluminum cookie sheet. Using a sharp knife, she scored the rounded dough into eight triangular sections, then popped it into the preheated oven to bake. The air smelled good, much like a bakery at dawn.

On the stove she filled a hunter-green kettle with cold water. While it boiled, she filled a stainless steel tea ball with loose cinnamon-orange tea. She took her favorite ceramic pot, a peach seashell shape, from a tall cupboard over the sink, rinsed it and set the filled tea ball inside just in time to take the hot kettle off the stove.

She poured the steamy hot water over the cool metal tea ball, returned the empty kettle to the stove, put the lid on the teapot, then put the teapot on a glossy wicker serving tray, a favored tray the color of honey. Prior to mixing the scones, she had laid a hand-crocheted doily on the serving tray, a matching crystal sugar and creamer, homemade strawberry jam, and a silver jam spoon.

The food she smelled joined forces with the silence

she needed to heal her flagged spirit although she couldn't completely escape the nagging thoughts about the identity of Mary Lou's secret love and Minette's strange behavior on Dessert Night. Could it be that she was involved with Hurley?

These thoughts briefly disappeared when she carried the wicker serving tray to the sun room. Kicking off her worn leather loafers, she placed the tray on the coffee table, a table scattered with the latest magazines: *Black Enterprise, Ebony, Essence, Heart and Soul,* and *Jet.*

She lit the three mint-colored candles sitting on the coffee table, ornaments that matched the flowers on the creamy background of the teapot. The teapot matched the teacup and saucer, all complemented with sterling cutlery reserved for private moments like this, moments of spiritual nurturing.

Bailey's grandmother said some people called this divine restoration a connection to the Creator, Christ, God, Buddha, Nature, or Allah. Bailey simply considered this spiritual time a means of connecting with the universe, a means of celebrating her infinitesimal role within eternity.

At the ringing of the kitchen timer, she bee-lined to the double oven, donned her teddy bear oven mitts, and removed the scones. The bread smelled divine, if Bailey had to say so herself, so divine she almost could not wait to slowly slice it. Careful to follow the indentations she had made on the fragrant dough before it baked, she sliced the hot, buttery bread into eight large pieces.

In the silent sun room, feeling far better now than when she first began baking, Bailey sat on the wicker couch and savored the first slice of her oven-hot scones. She experienced no interruptions and stared at the deep velvet sky, a sky lighted everywhere by millions of brilliant stars.

With her stress disappearing and her mouth well into the second scone, an unwelcome commotion penetrated Bailey's languor. It was Minette, a very angry-looking Minette with Sam trailing fast on her heels.

"Sorry, Bailey," he apologized while he stared angrily at Minette. "I told her you didn't want visitors, but she said she had to speak to you."

Pushing her tray aside, Bailey sat up. "It's all right, Sam," she assured him. "I think I know what she wants to talk about."

When Sam reluctantly left, Minette stared at Bailey for minutes before she spoke. "Hurley called me. He said you put the police on him. Why?" she demanded, her eyes glittering.

Bailey measured a long, lingering look at Minette, a look that found the woman lacking. Whatever happened to honor among friends? she wondered. "I told the police what I felt they needed to know in order to ensure my family's safety. I would think you'd want the same thing. Why do you care so much about Hurley?" she asked, though she suspected she knew the answer.

Minette let the criticism roll off her conscience like salad oil on a boiled egg. "I'm sorry about your assault. Knowing you accused Hurley of the crime made me angry. I work with him, Bailey, and I don't see him as a criminal."

"Is the reason you don't see him as a criminal because he's your lover?" she asked, remembering again how proud Minette had seemed of the way Hurley arranged Mary Lou's funeral events.

Minette froze. "How . . . did you . . . know?"

"I started wondering ever since Dessert Night about who your mystery man is, especially after all that gossip about Mary Lou's affair. Neither of you wanted anyone to know who you were seeing. I wondered why."

Minette inhaled a deep, shaky breath before sitting down. "Tell me."

Bailey studied Minette with an open expression. "You told me you were still seeing Judd. Also, that he continued to hurt you. Being a private person in a very public profession, you'd need to see a doctor for your injuries who was handy and discreet. What better doctor than Hurley Booker, a man who'd want to keep his private business as under wraps as you would?"

Minette rallied. "It could have been anyone."

"But it wasn't," Bailey said, shaking her head. By not denying the charge, Minette had confirmed her recent suspicions. "When I told you I don't recall Mary Lou going on and on about Hurley in the same way she talked about Cambria, you hinted they weren't happy. You came up with reasons for his rude behavior. When I said he was remote, you countered with possible shock. When I asked you what he was like at work, you didn't stick to vague words like *nice* or *respected*. Those would be common terms used for a casual coworker. You said he was analytic, perceptive, knowledgeable. When we talked about Hurley, or Mary Lou and Hurley, you were tense. And finally, you refused to give the name of your lover, which you normally would. It didn't fit until tonight."

Minette's face was stricken. "Your intuition has always been strong. You're right. About everything."

"What happened, Minette?" Bailey asked, her voice soft and compelling. She wondered how her friend could be so savvy in her career yet so misguided in her choice of men.

"I started seeing Hurley professionally because of what Judd had done. One night I thought my ribs were cracked. I'm so well known in northern California hospitals, I'd have to be discreet for the kind of medical care I needed. An accident as an excuse will work only twice. So I called Hurley at his office, asked him to meet me at my house, and the rest is history."

Bailey's lips were pressed together with disappointment. "How could you betray Mary Lou?"

"I didn't mean to. It just . . . happened. I needed a shoulder to lean on. Hurley's was it."

Bailey sighed, aware that both her friends had lived secret, yet parallel lives. "I can't believe you, Minette. Not only were you dating a friend's husband, you were dating a prominent married doctor at your own hospital. Either way you played with fire."

Minette nervously wet her lips with the tip of her tongue. "It was over between Hurley and me when Mary Lou died. I've been very upset by the whole thing. What I can't believe is that you think Hurley murdered his wife."

Bailey's temper climbed. Since she had not called Minette about the attack, it meant Hurley had called her after his visit by Detective Williams. This meant Minette's relationship was not completely over, as Minette wanted her to believe. "Mary Lou's mother, Yolanda, suspects Hurley of wrongdoing, too."

The skin on the back of Minette's neck prickled. "Why?"

Bailey paused, wondering if she should continue. In the end, she decided Minette could be in danger without knowing it. "She told me Mary Lou and Hurley were having trouble in their marriage. She wasn't pleased, but she wasn't surprised to hear Mary Lou may have been having an affair. Because Mary Lou mentioned Hurley was seeing a woman from his workplace, she suspected Mary Lou started an affair as revenge. Do you know whom she was seeing, Minette?"

Minette stood up rapidly, then paced the room, running her hands through her bangs again and again. She said nothing.

Bailey was concerned by her friend's rapid shift in behavior, the reason her body tensed with trepidation. "Minette?"

Minette dropped down once more beside Bailey on the wicker couch. Her shoulders were slumped, her expression grim. "She was seeing Judd. And it wasn't the first time, either. She'd dated him during his *captain player* days. When she found out I was seeing Hurley, she went for my jugular by going after Judd."

"What!"

"I'm saying, Bailey, that Mary Lou started seeing Judd because she wanted to get back at me for dating her husband. Mary Lou and I argued bitterly."

Bailey was aghast. "Yet you continued to see Hurley?"

Minette's response was low. "Because she continued to see Judd. I was jealous."

"Minette!"

"Even though Judd and I were divorced, I didn't want Mary Lou to have what was once . . . mine."

Bailey gripped her friend's forearms. "Don't you see, Minette?"

"See what?"

Bailey's eyes bored into Minette's. "Mary Lou's affair could have been Hurley's motive for murder."

Minette's skin crawled. "No. I can't see it."

"Detective Williams believes my theory that Mary Lou was murdered carries weight. That was the reason he visited Hurley."

Minette's head ached. "Tell me about the attack," she intoned softly.

Bailey did. She included her theory that Hurley only meant to scare the living daylights out of her.

Nervous at the news, Minette bit her lip. Hurley's opinion did not coincide with Bailey's clear rendition of events. "You can't be sure it was him."

"I'm sure it was a man by the way he felt, his strength, and the quality of his voice."

Minette shook her head. "I don't believe Hurley would . . . risk his reputation. Besides, he said he was on his way to Providence Hospital to perform a medical procedure at the time of your attack."

Bailey argued the point. "We don't live far from the hospital, Minette, and the attack lasted only brief minutes. There was time." Time enough to kill her too, she thought with a shudder.

Minette reached for a still-warm scone. For the life of her she did not understand why Bailey didn't weigh four hundred pounds because of the serious good food she liked to make. "I find it hard to believe that Hurley,

a physician, would be so cold he'd force his wife overboard ship."

"I can't believe you were dating Mary Lou's husband."

"You don't understand," Minette countered. She extended her hand.

Bailey looked at Minette's hand before taking it.
Even though she was angry and hurt by her friend's
actions, she believed in Minette's basic goodness. "Try
me."

Minette's eyes were misty as she squeezed Bailey's
fingers, welcoming the sister-girlfriend thread that connected them, even through tragedy. "Everything between me and Hurley was so innocent at first. I was
crying, happy my ribs were bruised not broken, sad because my private life was a wreck. Somehow we ended
up holding each other. He felt . . . strong. I needed that
strength."

Bailey shook her head, her voice sincere. "You've
got to make up your mind, Minette. Either you're with
Hurley. Or you're with me."

Minette's loyalty to Hurley and Bailey was at a
crossroads. She was between a rock and a hard place.
Hurley was an attentive lover, while Bailey was a long-
time friend. Yes, she decided. She knew all about
cracks, being in one at that precise moment—an emotional crack, one in which she wrestled between a
known good, Bailey, and a potential evil, Hurley.

It was a pivotal point between a troubled, frag-
mented past and a positive future, one she wanted to
someday share with a decent and loving man like Sam.
Minette reached a decision, her shoulders squared.
"I'm with you. Over the years you've never wanted

anything for me but my happiness. Even now, when you could be screaming and cursing, you're compassionate." Minette wiped her eyes. "I'll help you any way I can. If Hurley's innocent, the truth will prove it."

Bailey wanted to believe her. "Are you serious, Minette?"

"Very."

Bailey hugged her. "Hurley called here after the police questioned him. He wanted to speak openly about my accusation."

"Do the police know he called you?"

"Not yet. With Sam here I feel safe."

"Why did you agree to the meeting if you suspect Hurley of assault and murder?"

"Suspect him is right," Bailey confirmed. "I don't have proof, information he might divulge in a loose moment while speaking to me. With the police conscious of my suspicion, he isn't likely to behave in a risky way. I want to hear what he has to say, which might be more than he would say in front of the police."

Minette tapped her foot against the floral throw rug at her feet. "To tell you the truth, as soon as Hurley told me about your accusations, I charged over here like a fool to defend his character. He was very good to me, Bailey. If he did plan to murder Mary Lou, I was primed to defend his character as I did tonight, saying he isn't capable of such a cold-hearted crime. Even though I don't like the idea of Hurley being a suspect, I discourage you from holding anything back from the police."

"I won't."

Minette sighed, her shoulder muscles tense, her mind cluttered with regret at the current unpleasant ripple in their lives. Any other time, tea in Bailey's moon-dappled sun room would anesthetize tension. On this night, she wanted a Valium instead of herbal tea. "I didn't know you're such a risk taker, Bailey," she observed.

Bailey riveted her guarded gaze to a dangling spider-web on the sloped-glass ceiling, thinking she needed to set aside a day for cobweb cleaning. "The sooner we discover the truth, the sooner our lives will return to normal."

"Amen," Minette breathed.

When Hurley arrived at nine-thirty that night, Minette was long gone. Fern was asleep. "I'm sorry for the lateness of the hour. I'm on-call at the hospital," he apologized.

Bailey waved a hand toward a chair in the living room. "Sit down," she offered, glad her husband was nearby. Sam was not in the mood for pleasantries. He stood rigid, establishing his power and protective nature. His lips were tight, his arms akimbo. They had decided to let Bailey do the talking, Sam providing the physical backup.

Austere and still in the suit he had worn all day, Hurley declined the offer to sit. "Homicide Detective Williams says you think I attacked you today. What's going on, Bailey?"

"I believe Mary Lou was murdered."

"You think I did it?"

Bailey sized him up, thinking, imagining, reasoning. "Yes."

Hurley crossed his arms. "Why?"

Bailey looked him in the eye. "You tell me."

Hurley's eyes grew small. He ran an agitated hand over the back of his head. He did it once. He did it twice. "Look, I don't want to believe Mary Lou killed herself either. She did."

Bailey lifted a brow. "I was attacked today. The man believed I had something that Mary Lou gave me. You're the only man I can think of who might think Mary Lou would hide anything with me."

"Did she?"

"No. Now I've got a question for you. Did you know she was having an affair?"

Coldly furious, Hurley looked her in the eye. "Yes."

Bailey didn't miss the unresolved anger. "For how long?"

Hurley considered not answering. "Long enough."

Bailey pressed him. "Did you confront her?"

"Yes," he admitted.

"And?" she prompted.

"Mary Lou laughed in my face, telling me I'm a cold fish and cold fish need traitors like my lover, Minette. Mary Lou demanded a divorce." Hurley spat the last word out.

This was news to Bailey and she couldn't hide her shock. "What did you tell her?"

Hurley crackled hot and angry. "I told her no, and suggested we seek counseling."

Bailey leaned forward, all her senses alert, unable to picture Hurley telling all to a therapist. "Yolanda

Perkins said Mary Lou wasn't above an affair for revenge. That meant you were cheating first. Were you?"

Hurley grunted. "Mary Lou didn't understand. Minette was convenient."

Bailey studied Hurley for a tense moment. "You're talking double standards here, Hurley. You had an affair with Minette. Your wife found out, cheated on you, which you couldn't stand, so you killed her. Is that right, Hurley?" She asked him point-blank, her tone unforgiving. She would never have been so bold had Sam not been standing by to protect her. She was also comforted knowing Detective Williams had taken her suspicions seriously enough to act on them right away.

Hurley glanced at Sam and noticed he just stood there, bold and intimidating. "Do you honestly believe I'm going to admit to murder? I came here to tell you to keep my name out of your messy problems. I didn't attack you today and I don't know why you're telling lies to the police about me." Hurley was hoarse with raw anger.

Sam was furious himself. "Listen, Booker," he said, casting a frigid, measured look over every inch of Hurley's large body. "Even if Mary Lou wasn't murdered, something ugly was going on in your house. The police are suspicious now, which means the truth, good or bad, will come out eventually."

Hurley laughed at that, a harsh sound. "You just keep me out of your crazy business." He turned to leave, but Sam stopped him with a grip on the shoulder.

"Don't come here again, Booker," he warned, his tone hard and ominous, his eyes level. "I protect what's mine. Remember that."

* * *

After locking the door behind Hurley, Sam walked over to where Bailey stood in the foyer, watching him. "It's been a hell of a day. First you were attacked. Then Minette's visit. And now Hurley's. Minette and Mary Lou led secret, overlapping lives. I wonder what else we don't know."

"So do I."

Sam frowned. "How's your throat?"

"Better." Much of her fear had been replaced with a solid will to get to the bottom of what happened to Mary Lou.

"I'm glad. Did Minette ask you about it?" he queried, softly stroking the bruise.

"No. She came here to defend Hurley. We ended up talking about the affairs between her and Hurley and Mary Lou and Judd. To tell you the truth, I wasn't thinking about my throat either."

"And now?"

She went into his arms, her cheek against his chest. "I want some comfort."

"My pleasure."

Inside their bedroom, Sam lit a single ivory candle. The only music they listened to was the sound of each other's breathing. Soft as warm, gentle rain, Sam's fingers eased through the red-brown thickness of Bailey's hair. He massaged her scalp with strong fingers, then her shoulders.

"You've got magic hands," she complimented him, her breathing mellow as she began to relax. Her back was against his chest, his hard body long and virile against her softer one. "I can't tell you how much it means to have you at home. It makes me feel safe."

"I'll always be here for you."

Bailey turned within his arms to embrace his waist. "Honey, let's make love. Slowly."

"You read my mind." Tasting the tips of her ear-lobes, Sam slipped his tongue along their edges. Her shivers of delight quickened his pulse.

Bailey wished that the world were as perfect as the candle that cast its light around them like a flower of flame. In the privacy of their bedroom she thought it was right for them to take from an imperfect life what they truly wanted, especially when what they wanted was each other.

Sam greeted this fresh chance to continue the potent magic he began with his wife on their wedding day. Wrapping an arm about her waist, he led her to their canopied bed. The lone ivory candle, a symbol of their unity, spangled the somnolent bedroom with mysterious and fluttering shadows as they explored each other with lazy, luscious need.

Bailey had only to sigh softly and sweetly in order to ignite Sam further. When she supplemented those sweet sighs by opening her admiring arms, her limber legs, and her sterling mind to him, he eagerly accepted every aspect of what she willingly gave, thus doing his special part to replenish their physical and spiritual alliance. Their love was an unbreakable bond between them, one strengthened by the need to mend after that day's emotional events.

Nine

Friday morning was vibrant and clear. Bailey sat with Sam, drinking coffee at the nook as they waited for Fern to join them at the table. Bailey wore double-pleated tan dress slacks with a cream silk blouse. Sam wore tapered black slacks with a slate-gray band shirt. They had arranged a meeting with Mr. and Mrs. Perkins regarding Bailey's attack and the key they had found behind Mary Lou's kitchen switch-plate.

"Is Fern always this slow in the morning before school? Sam asked, after waiting ten minutes for her to arrive for breakfast.

"Only in the last weeks of school. She's ready for summer break."

Sam touched Bailey's shoulder. "Ready for our adventure today?

"What adventure?" Fern asked as she moseyed into the kitchen, her favorite place in the house besides her bedroom. Her mother always had something delicious to eat tucked away. On that morning it was warm pumpkin-spice muffins and orange juice.

"The adventure of discovery," Bailey answered as she took in her daughter's attire, cobalt-colored denims and a magenta cotton top. "I believe we're a breath away from very big news."

Curious, Fern peered close at her parents' faces. "About Cambria's mom?" she asked, wanting to get in on the interesting conversation.

"Yes." Sam and Bailey knew children often picked up more than grown-ups thought they did. "We'll explain it all to you after we get our news."

Bailey knelt to eye level with her daughter. "We found a key of Mary Lou's we want her mother to have. We plan to visit her this morning."

Fern twirled a long thick braid about one finger, obviously nervous. "Mom. Daddy. Cambria gave me a secret."

Maternal instincts to the fore, Bailey zeroed in on her daughter. "What kind of secret?"

"A box."

Thrusting his broad nose six inches shy of his daughter's narrow one, Sam stated firmly, "You know full well you're never to keep secrets from us, Fern Walker."

Nervous, Fern squirmed. "I know, Daddy, but Cambria was real scared, so I helped her. She's my friend."

"How did you sneak a box past me, Fern?" Bailey asked, stunned.

Even though Fern was nervous, she was not afraid of her parents because she knew they loved her unconditionally. "Cambria gave me a box at school. She said to hide it."

Sam sighed heavily. "Tell us everything, Fern. Leave nothing out."

Torn between obeying her father and breaking her promise to Cambria, Fern was not certain what to do. Her indecision disturbed Sam because he suddenly realized his baby girl was not a baby anymore and was making decisions on her own. He tried to keep the stern look squarely on his face.

When at last Fern spoke, it was with great care, just like her father. "Cambria gave me the box at school and told me to hide it. I put it in my backpack. When I got home, I put it in my old doll buggy. The pink one."

"But why?" Bailey asked.

"Cambria told me her mom and dad were fussing at each other a lot and her mom didn't want Mr. Hurley to have what was in the box." Fern spoke quickly, running the words together as if a burden had been lifted from her.

Sam placed a hand on Fern's shoulder. "What's in the box?"

"Don't know."

"Okay," Sam said, his attitude serious yet loving. "First of all, I appreciate your honesty. Second, I want to see that box."

Emotion-torn, Fern felt a little guilty about breaking her secret with Cambria. Even though she wanted to help her parents, she wanted to help her friend, too. "Daddy, I promised Cambria."

Bailey looked between father and daughter. They wore the same stubborn set of jaw. "You've already told us where the box is, Fern. Either you get it now, or one of us will."

Still hesitant, Fern struggled again with her guilt-ridden conscience. "Okay, Mom. I'll get it."

Watching his daughter stride away, Sam could only stare in amazement. He appreciated her struggle between duty and desire, her duty to her parents and her desire to protect her friend, a duty much like the one

Bailey experienced for Mary Lou. "I hope she eventually understands she did the right thing," he told his wife.

Bailey smiled, serene in a mother's keen understanding. "Oh, she knows she did the right thing. She just doesn't like it."

When Fern returned, she reluctantly handed the box to her father. Sam handed it to Bailey, then hunkered down to Fern's size. "Sugar, no matter what you say or what you do, mommy and I will always love you. I'm glad you told us about the box. It took a lot of courage to tell us about the secret."

Fern threw her arms around her father's neck, squeezing so hard, he had trouble breathing. "Okay," she said, as Sam hugged her back. He kissed the end of her nose.

Bailey smiled at them. "If we don't hurry, you'll be late for school. Your class is having a popcorn party at lunchtime right?"

"Oh, yeah," Fern remembered, pleasure in her voice.

Sam tousled her braids. "Grandma was asking if you'd like to spend the night at her house later? Want to go?"

Bouncing up and down, Fern was already glowing with excitement. Her daddy's mother loved to shop. So did Fern. "Yep."

Sam grinned. "Good. When mommy and I pick you up from school today, we'll have an early dinner before taking you to Grandma's."

"Okay, but, Daddy?"

"Yes, sugar?"

"What're you gonna do with the box?"

"Give it to Cambria's grandmother when we visit

this morning." Squeezing Fern one more time, he added, "Now, eat your breakfast. It's almost time to go."

Once Fern was dropped off at school, Bailey and Sam beat it home to open the box Cambria had entrusted to her. It was a gray metal square with a lock and no key. Sam looked at Bailey. Bailey looked at Sam. "The switch-plate key," they uttered in unison, excitement evident in both their eyes as they carried the box from the nook to their bedroom, where the key was hidden.

Bailey pulled the switch-plate key from her own hiding place, a slim box of thigh-high black stockings. Almost reverent, she set the box in the center of the bed she shared every night with Sam. With trembling fingers she slid the cold metal key inside the equally cold lock. It was a perfect fit. Her breath held in anticipation, she lifted the steel lid slowly, as if the contents inside would vanish should the lamplight shine upon it in a blazing rush. Inside the slick square box were compromising photographs of Hurley with a variety of women.

Sam was stunned, glad they shared the suspense of solving the puzzling mystery behind Mary Lou's death together. Had Bailey not been suspicious about the suicide, the reason she had stuck her nose in Hurley Booker's business, he didn't know when they would have discovered Fern and Cambria possessed the metal box. "The rotten motives behind friendly faces are spooky," he murmured.

"Very," Bailey agreed.

Sam assessed his wife, then steepled his fingers before him as he sat on the edge of their pillow-packed bed. "I've given a lot of thought to projected images of late. Take Cambria, for instance. Until now we assumed her innocent of corruption because of her youth, but she knew something was wrong. She lied. Remember what she did through Fern."

Bailey didn't want to believe it either, didn't want to think about it, but she did. She scooted away from the middle of the bed to sit next to Sam, her right thigh touching his left one. "I've considered Cambria only as a victim, not as part of this puzzle," she admitted, her mind reluctant to accept the notion. "Because of Mary Lou's death, I've been stuck on her motherless state. It never occurred to me she'd be the recipient of the possible source of her mother's murder."

Sam cracked his knuckles, something he did when he felt flustered. "It makes me wonder how much Cambria truly knows. Maybe Mrs. Perkins can find out."

Bailey mulled the suggestion over, then shook her head. "Cambria didn't trust her grandmother with the locked box to begin with. Maybe she doesn't trust the adults in her life, adults we'd take for granted she should trust. The person Cambria trusted most was Fern, another child," she pointed out. "The children were smart enough to know something stinks among the adults in their lives. It's probably the reason the steel box was kept a secret."

Sam shifted his weight on the bed, anger bubbling up to the surface. "Fern's been in grave danger all along. We just didn't know it." He forced the words through tight lips.

Bailey squeezed his knee, a gesture of comfort. "Taking her to your mother's after school is good. She'll be safe."

Sam's hands clinched into fists. "Yesterday when you called to tell me about your attack, I was shocked and angry. I could only wonder if you were hurt or scared. I wanted to kill whoever touched you."

"I'm okay. And now the police are involved."

Sam flexed his wrists. "Know something?"

"What?"

"For all her peaceful ways, Mary Lou had a mean streak."

Bailey agreed. "She actually flaunted her relationship with Judd every time she came to Dessert Night, but no one ever knew what she was doing except for Minette."

"Who is calculated herself," Sam added.

"Why do you say that?"

Sam explained. "I don't believe a woman as young as she is makes it to the top of her career without being single-minded in her desire to achieve goals. Minette is ambitious. So is Hurley."

Bailey considered the possibilities. "Hurley and Judd are alike as well. Both men are successful in their respective careers; Hurley as a lung specialist, Judd as a contractor. They are men in business for themselves. Both men have a love-hate complex about beautiful, successful women that pushes them to behave in intimidating ways in private. Hurley beat Mary Lou's emotions. Judd beat Minette's body. What both men have in common is a latent cruelty toward women that rears its head when the men feel their power is usurped in any way."

Sam wrinkled his brow as he analyzed what he'd heard. "One similarity between Hurley and Judd is the depth of their cruelty. When Judd hurt Minette, he came back, apologizing. He must have been genuine, because she believed they could work their problems out. Part of this belief was based on their original love for each other. Hurley used verbal abuse. It's a cleaner form of violence than battery because there is no physical evidence. His manner is cold and calculating, the way I expect his thinking to be."

Sam was decisive. "We need answers. It's the only way I see him being prosecuted for murder."

At ten o'clock Sam pulled the minivan in front of Yolanda Perkins's home, Bailey at his side. The charming one-story house was painted a medium blue with rose trim. Twin stands of potted Boston fern sat on either side of the stained-glass windowed oak door. There were two sedans in the driveway, a silver Honda and a platinum Oldsmobile. Sam knocked on the door, every nerve alert.

Mrs. Perkins greeted them with open arms, ushering them quickly into the house. Her husband, Adam, stood beside her, his expression intent. Like Sam, he was present to protect his family.

"I'm so glad you came," Yolanda stated, her voice filled with pleasure. "Now, tell us. What's going on?"

"Hold it, Yoli," Adam said as he offered Sam his hand. Adam Perkins was fifty-two-years-old. At five-feet-ten-inches he looked healthy and fit. The gray at his temples added distinguishing features to a nut-brown, intelligent, and dimpled face. He encased his stocky frame in a tan business suit.

Once Yolanda released Bailey from a fierce motherly hug, Bailey assessed her. At five-feet-three-inches, she was plump in all the right places. Her cinnamon-colored skin was smooth and blemish-free. Smelling like Chanel No. 5, she wore a plum jacquard dress. Like Adam, she couldn't take her eyes of the metal box Sam carried.

Adam spoke first. "We can open the box in the living room. Yoli's got coffee and tea waiting on a serving cart."

Everyone settled in. Sam and Bailey on the Queen Anne love seat. Adam and Yolanda sat on the matching sofa.

"I don't believe it!" Yolanda exclaimed, after Bailey told them what happened since they first spoke on the telephone. "You say Cambria gave the box to your daughter?"

"Yes," Bailey answered.

"And you were attacked yesterday?" Adam confirmed, obviously disturbed by the news.

Sam responded, grim. "We believe it was Hurley."

Adam Perkins clenched his fists. "I'm don't believe—"

"Now, wait, Adam," Yolanda interrupted, her throaty voice primed to calm him down as she put a hand on his forearm. "We said we'd let the police handle Hurley. There's no sense in you going to jail, too."

Adam's expression was filled with hate. "I want to—"

"Adam." Yolanda's single soft-spoken word silenced the grief-stricken, furious father.

Adam cleared his throat. "Tell us about the box and key."

Sam did. And Adam sighed. "My daughter was cunning."

"Adam!"

He patted his wife's knee. "She was, Yoli. She was tough, too. She wanted the prestige of being a rich man's wife, we knew that. She knew every doctor wasn't rich, but she knew Hurley would be rich eventually, due to his ambition. If she was a trophy wife, he was a trophy husband. I felt sorry for Cambria."

"Adam!"

Adam spoke quietly and firmly. "I did, Yoli. I still do. I know Mary Lou was devoted to that child more than anybody except you and me. But she had a wild hair and you know it."

"Adam Elija Perkins, you watch your mouth. You know our daughter was good." Yolanda twisted her fingers together in her lap.

Adam placed his hands over hers, calming their flustered movement. "She was good, Yoli, but she had her bad side, too. When did you ever know Mary Lou to pick her friends, her clothes, her wants, without thinking about them first? Whatever she had or wanted, it was the best."

Yolanda said nothing for a while. Then she sighed heavily. She looked at Sam, then Bailey and stated proudly, "I loved my daughter. She was warm and good and kind. At least she was as long as things were going her way."

A muscle flickered in Bailey's jaw. "Hurley says she wanted a divorce."

Adam snorted. "That's a lie. He wanted one from

her, only she didn't want it. She said she put in too many years with him to let some other woman reap her rewards."

Sam was puzzled. "Why would he lie?"

Adam countered. "Why would he kill her? Lord knows they'd been cheating on each other off and on for years. Every time Mary Lou found out he was fooling around on her, she cut loose with somebody herself just to spite him."

Yolanda squeezed Adam's hand as if seeking strength. "You've got to understand. They did love each other. At least in the beginning. It was plain to see then. When Hurley started getting more successful, Mary Lou resented it. The more successful Hurley became, the more time he spent away from home. Somehow she found out about his affairs. That's how the tit-for-tat started between them. He'd have one, she'd have one, and so on."

Bailey could understand why Yolanda would edit her first opinions to her over the telephone. The rivalry and revenge pattern going on between Mary Lou and Hurley was as ugly as it was private. "Why do you think she went to such lengths to hide these items?"

Adam's mouth thinned with displeasure. "Knowing the games Mary Lou and Hurley played, I bet she wanted him to find that stuff after she made him crazy tracking it down. Like I said before, my daughter was cunning, good, and bad. My guess is something happened between Hurley and Mary Lou that they couldn't get over. Now one of them is dead. I just wish it were that damned Hurley."

Sam shook his head. "I just wish the two of them

had been sensible and parted ways instead of playing games. Sometimes I don't understand people."

Adam leveled a look at Sam. "The trick to getting along with people is accepting who they are, not who you want them to be. Maybe Yoli and I can do right by Cambria. We sure want to try."

Bailey hoped so. "We need to tell the police about our findings."

Yolanda reached toward an end table where a telephone rested. "You're right. Call that detective you told us about. Tell him to meet us here."

Detective Ridge Williams appeared at Yolanda and Adam Perkins' home within twenty minutes of Sam's telephone call. Dashing and handsome, his teeth flashed politely at everyone present when Adam escorted him in. Ridge's brow was furrowed with concern. "You two are fortunate you weren't hurt," he chastised Sam and Bailey regarding their breaking and entering antics on Daisy Lane.

Sam understood his concern. "We were careful."

Removing his mechanical pencil and notepad from an inner pocket of his single-breasted camel-colored suit, the detective asked, "What did you find, exactly?"

Sam told him.

"Compromising photos of Hurley with other women." There was a critical tone in Sam's voice.

"It's not exactly legal . . . so we need a confession," the detective decided. "Since you've done all this legwork on your own, I suspect you have a plan in mind for Hurley Booker."

Bailey looked at each person in the room. "I have a plan. We need Minette to pull it off."

The detective returned his mechanical pencil and notepad to his inner breast suit pocket. "Call her."

Dressed in olive slacks and a matching sweater, Minette expected her guest to arrive at her town house within minutes. It was noon. Sam and Detective Williams waited in the guest room off the foyer, pending a cue from Bailey or Minette to join them. When the bell rang, Minette opened the door. Hurley Booker walked in, looking dark and forbidding in a brass buttoned navy blazer with matching slacks and a mock blue turtleneck.

"What's the deal?" he asked Minette, his voice cold, his eyes narrowed to slits as his eyes swept maliciously across Bailey.

"We have . . . proof you killed Mary Lou," Minette responded.

Hurley laughed with his voice, but not his eyes. Something wicked crackled and snapped inside them because they were as deadly as his voice was ominous. Bailey's probing hadn't been healthy for his image. "What's your proof?"

Bailey answered this time. "Photos."

Hurley studied her slowly, his mind whirling. He spoke distinctly. "If you think I killed Mary Lou, what makes you think I won't kill you, too?"

When Bailey didn't say anything, Hurley started looking around. "Where's Sam?"

"I'm right here," Sam answered, striding into the

living room. Detective Williams remained in the guest room, not wanting to throw Hurley off until necessary.

Hurley's eyes registered an obsidian hate. The hate lived and breathed as he whipped out a menacing revolver from the small of his sweaty back. "I'll kill the lot of you," he announced, his tone malicious.

"You can't kill us all, Hurley. Give it up," Minette warned, shocked by his vehemence. She'd never seen him so intense and hostile.

Sweat slipped off his body in beads. Hurley's carefully laid plans were unraveling like twine around him, something he could do little about. The lack of control disturbed his cold, orderly, competent way of life. He liked control.

"She's telling the truth," Sam enjoined. "The only thing left to figure out is why. Why did you murder Mary Lou?"

Hurley fondled the trigger as he debated spouting off details. In the end he determined he had nothing to lose. "I'd always wondered why Cambria didn't look like me. But, since she was a girl and had so many of Mary Lou's features, I chucked it up to fate, believing what I wanted to believe—that Cambria was mine."

"What are you talking about?" Bailey asked.

But he continued as if she had not spoken. "I married Mary Lou because she was everything I'm not. She was beautiful. She created lovely things. More than any other woman, she saw my potential, stuck by me, focused on being an asset. She was a superb hostess, stunning in dress, thought, and speech. I appreciated it all. I even acknowledge I may not be as successful as I am today had it not been for Mary Lou's quiet yet firm manipulations on the business front.

"As long as she kept her affairs private, I didn't care. We were both discreet. I'd do it when I met someone I really liked. She did the same. I preferred married women or women who weren't looking for a permanent relationship. She chose men from out of town, usually San Francisco or Oakland. Two months ago we were fighting and she told me about Cambria. She'd discovered I was seeing Minette when a private investigator took photos of us leaving a hotel room together in Santa Cruz. Mary Lou went crazy.

"She told me she and Judd had met before she and I were married. She met Minette through Bailey when we moved to Daisy Lane three years ago, but Mary Lou never said anything about her relationship with Judd until she found out I was seeing Minette. She told me about Cambria in a fit of rage during an argument, one of many that came to a head on the pleasure cruise. There was no way I could live with her anymore and no way I could let her go and face ridicule by the disclosure of Cambria's paternity. Cambria is eight-years-old, but I didn't know she wasn't mine until just weeks ago.

"I've worked hard to gain a prominent position at Providence Hospital and in New Hope. I wasn't about to have that image ruined by the sordid details of Mary Lou's indiscretion. Her initial affair with Judd lasted just long enough for her to get pregnant by mistake. She said the condom he used broke. I find that hard to believe, but that's the reason she gave me. I never questioned Cambria's paternity, because at the time, we hadn't started tit-for-tat, as she called it. At least, that's what I'd thought until recently. The idea she'd been using me, that I was cuckolded, was unbearable. I wanted her dead, so I killed her."

Minette's eyes were dazed and she looked ill, her expression stricken. "You buffaloed everyone. Who'd expect a prominent and respected physician to be a cold-blooded killer?"

Hurley laughed, a maniacal sound. The muscle beneath his left eye twitched and pulsed with acute tension. "Have I ever treated you coldly?"

"No. And it scares me to no end," Minette admitted softly. "It scares me to know that underneath your civil exterior lies the heart and soul of a savage."

"So you admit it?" Bailey confirmed for the record. The small tape recorder on a bookshelf keeping track of every word.

"Yes, I admit it. I killed Mary Lou and I'm not sorry. I hated her, loved her, and needed her, too. People loved Mary Lou because of her beauty, talent, and wit. She enhanced my social position, embellished me with a grace I didn't possess on my own. With her I could accomplish just about anything. I was fine with our life until she told me about Cambria."

"You're saying you aren't Cambria's father? And that's why Mary Lou died?"

"Exactly."

"But you raised Cambria, you—"

"Were cuckolded! Judd Ramsey is Cambria's father!"

Minette collapsed on the couch.

"Why didn't you kill Judd, too?" Sam asked.

"He didn't know about Cambria nor was he involved in her life. Cambria's paternity was Mary Lou's best kept secret."

"And what about Cambria?"

"When Mary Lou slipped and told me about Cambria, she begged me not to do something rash that would hurt the child. I promised Mary Lou I wouldn't hurt Cambria. Betrayed as I feel, I do still love her. I couldn't destroy her innocence. Sending her to live with Yolanda solved the problem of raising her, knowing she wasn't mine. But Mary Lou outfoxed me, didn't she? She left clues for anybody who'd care to find them. I wonder if she suspected it might be you, Bailey. She always said you were a tough cookie. I wanted to wring your blasted neck the day I entered your house through the kitchen nook door. I had looked everywhere for those photos, the only thing I could think of that might link me to something awry between me and Mary Lou."

Minette spoke up. "What about me? How did I fit into this mess, Hurley?"

Hurley the critic loomed to the fore. "You talk a lot about work, Minette. From you I learned the high-level and low-level machinations of every major hospital in Northern California. Where Mary Lou complemented my professional life on the domestic side, you complemented my professional life on the business side. Everything about you was strictly business."

"Even the sex?" she whispered.

"Especially the sex."

Minette was appalled. "You're sick, Hurley."

Disgusted, Sam asked, "What about your daughter?"

Hurley skewered Sam with sharp, assessing eyes. "She never was my daughter. Every time I look at her I'm reminded of what a fool I've been."

His weapon drawn, Detective Williams strode into the living room, making his presence known. "Hurley Booker, you're under arrest for murder," he stated coldly.

Stunned to hear another man's powerful voice, Hurley whipped around, anger and terror fighting for control in his eyes. The moment the detective appeared, Hurley recognized his career, his good name, and his dreams were dead: just like Mary Lou.

Desperate and more frustrated than he'd been in his entire life, Hurley roared, the sound as loud and ominous as rolling thunder. Beyond reason, his eyes narrowed, Hurley pointed the body-warmed barrel of his gun at Bailey. Had it not been for her, he'd be home free, safe on Flamingo Hill. He cocked the trigger.

Simultaneously, Sam lunged at Bailey, knocking her to the ground at the instant the detective fired a volley from his service revolver. Minette screamed, her fear stark and livid. As Bailey hit the floor, protected by Sam's length, she caught a glimpse of Hurley's falling, red-stained body. She knew, without being told, that justice had been served and that truth had prevailed for Mary Lou.

Tasty Treats on the Delicious Sweet Side

Chocolate Caramels
Applesauce Bars

Epilogue

It was Sunday in New Hope, a beautiful town with secrets so ugly that their revelation reminded Bailey how wealth, good health, and fortune were only part of the ingredients vital to living a good life. Selfless love, she decided, added spice to good living by creating a harmony between the mind, its body and its soul. Without this sacred ingredient, true happiness was only an illusion—as she'd discovered by delving into the mystery of Mary Lou Booker's death.

Wearing worn leather loafers, jeans, and a teal cotton top, Bailey hummed as she prepared enough delicious sweet treats to share with her neighbors: Jordanna's mother, Cora, and Mrs. MacAllister. Many neighbors didn't care what went on next door, but because these women did care, Bailey knew peace of mind.

Anticipating the healing activity of preparing good food for the people she loved, Bailey donned her red cotton apron over her jeans, tossed a thick tea towel over her shoulder, then cranked up an old Tower of Power tape on the boom box. For the chocolate caramel candy, she needed sugar, light cream, butter, corn syrup, unsweetened chocolate, salt, cream of tartar, and vanilla extract.

Once she placed the ingredients she needed on the

kitchen counter, she sprayed a handy metal pan with a non-stick food spray. Setting the pan aside, she combined the candy ingredients in a heavy saucepan, stirring the contents until the sugar dissolved. Standing at the pot while the ingredients came together served as a means of meditation for Bailey, a soothing time when the troubled thoughts of the recent past mellowed to manageable bits.

Minette had sold her town house. With weeks of psychotherapy behind her, she was on her way to a more balanced emotional life. Judd had agreed to clean up his abusive behavior by entering a rehab program for men who hurt the women in their lives. It was the only way Yolanda and Adam Perkins would allow him access to his daughter. Cambria and Fern played regularly with Jordanna. Hurley's will had left Cambria a very rich little girl. She was the only heir.

Once the chocolate caramel candy reached the smooth consistency she desired, Bailey poured the mixture into the prepared pan, where it would sit until hard enough to cut into bite-sized pieces. The tedious part of the candy-making process came when she'd need to wrap each piece in waxed paper, a familiar job she willingly shared with Fern, the official family sweet tooth. If Bailey loved baked goods, Fern loved sticky candy as much or more, the reason she sported two cavities.

Finished with the initial candymaking, Bailey prepared the second sweet treat, applesauce bars, a particular favorite of Sam's and Mrs. MacAllister's. Applesauce bars were tasteful treats that could be made with or without nuts. Sam liked them with nuts, Bailey without. Fern didn't care as long as she could eat them straight from the oven. Since she was cooking to relax, Bailey made them both ways, a pleasant event for the recipients of her positive energy, an energy put to good use in her humming country kitchen.

For the applesauce bars she needed flour, cinnamon, baking soda, salt, nutmeg, cloves, butter, vanilla, applesauce, raisins, and sugar. In a large bowl she creamed the sugar, vanilla, and butter. In a smaller bowl she sifted the dry ingredients which she alternated adding with the applesauce in the sugar-mixture bowl. This done, she tossed in plump brown raisins. The completed mixture went into a greased pan which she placed into a preheated oven until done. Once the cinnamon-spiced confection cooled, she would slice it into thick mouth-watering squares, a visual ambrosia.

Jazz music seeped slow and sanguine in the background as Sam entered the kitchen. Dressed in blue shorts and a gray tank top, he pulled Bailey close, so close he felt her heart beating against his chest. He could hear Fern playing with Jordanna in the backyard. Moments like these made him glad he'd traded his single life for a married one.

Bailey kissed his chin. "Have I told you today I'm grateful you're mine?"

"No." His teasing voice was deep and warm.

Bailey bit his lip. "Have I told you I love you?"

"Not lately, he bantered, rejoicing in having her snuggled tight against him.

Bailey cupped his face with gentle hands. "I love you, Sam. Thanks for being here."

Sam welcomed her fine faith, a deep and abiding commitment to their relationship. Feeling strong and protective, he brushed her inner ear with a whisper-soft kiss. "Mmm," he murmured, "paradise."

Bailey's Recipe Favorites

Fried Catfish

3 pounds of fish
Vegetable oil for frying
5 large eggs
2 cups flour
2 cups cornmeal
1 teaspoon salt
1 teaspoon pepper
2 tablespoons favorite spices

Warm oil for frying in a large skillet. While the oil is heating, beat the eggs in a medium-sized bowl. Mix the dry ingredients in a separate bowl. Put the dry ingredients in a brown paper bag. Coat the fish with the egg, then dredge it in the paper bag until coated well. Add the fish to the oil and fry until it looks a golden honey color. Drain the fish on paper towels. Serve with garnish on a pretty platter.

Okra Spread

1 pound of okra
4 cups water
1 garlic clove
1/2 onion
1 dash Tabasco
salt and pepper to taste
crackers

Put water in a large pot. Chop clove and onion, adding them to the pot. Add seasonings. Set the water mixture on medium. While the water warms, remove the stems and tips off the okra, slicing each piece into fourths. Place the okra in the pot. Bring okra mixture to a boil. Cook until all water is absorbed. Serve cold with crackers.

Black-eyed Pea Salad

1/2 bag of peas
1 piece of salt pork
1 onion
2 garlic cloves
3 celery ribs
1 tablespoon vinegar
3/4 teaspoon sugar
1/2 cup vegetable oil
salt and pepper to taste

Pick and soak peas overnight. Score salt pork, then boil it in a large pot to flavor the water. Toss the cleaned peas in the pot. Chop vegetables, then add half of them to the pot. Boil until peas are tender.

While the peas boil, prepare the vinegar dressing. In a glass bowl or large jar, toss oil, sugar, salt, pepper, plus remaining vegetables in the vinegar.

After the peas are tender, drain them well. Gently coat with vinegar mixture.

Waffles

1 package yeast
1/4 cup warm water
2 cups flour
1 teaspoon salt
2 tablespoons sugar
2 cups milk
3 eggs
1/4 cup vegetable oil
1 stick butter
favorite syrup

Soften yeast in water. Sift dry ingredients in large bowl. Add yeast, milk, oil, and eggs to dry ingredients. Combine until smooth. Cover bowl lightly to let mixture rise. When it doubles, stir it down. Refrigerate overnight in a covered container. Stir down again, adding a bit of milk if it's too thick. Brown batter in waffle iron. Top with butter and syrup.

Acknowledgments

Bettye Lewis, for teaching me how to cook from the heart.

Gearlune Moon, for the teatime tradition and other special memories.

Maythel Bolden, for showing me the trick to no-fail pie crusts.

Toni, for countless hours of Suzy Mary as kids. I love you, Sis.

Robin, I'm glad we found each other. Keep singing.

Dad, thanks for Albuquerque.

Karen, I treasured our mornings together.

Deborah, your enthusiasm inspired me.

Randal and Steve II, you make life delicious simply by being yourselves.

Steve, thanks for so many things. The computer. The patience. The love.

Dear Readers,

I love to cook for my family and friends, so that hobby combined naturally with my love for writing. *Delicious* is my first published book, one I hope you enjoyed reading. I welcome your thoughts regarding the story and ask that you mail your comments to the publisher who will then forward them to me. In turn, I'll write you back. Please include with your letter a business sized, self-addressed-stamped-envelope to:

Shelby Lewis
c/o Monica Harris, Editor
Kensington Publishing Corporation
850 Third Avenue
New York, NY 10022-6222

The idea of having readers respond to my stories is exciting. I look forward to hearing from you soon.

Sincerely,

Shelby Lewis

About the Author

Shelby Lewis lives in Northern California with her husband, Steve, and their young sons, Steven and Randal. An avid mystery and romance reader, Shelby enjoys black and white movie classics, flea market treasure hunting, baking, and lazing at the beach. *Delicious* is her first novel, the start of a food theme mystery series featuring amateur sleuths, Sam and Bailey Walker.

Dear Arabesque readers:

February is a month where we can celebrate the achievements of African-Americans and the joys of romance. This February we celebrate both in Arabesque.

Look for HOME FIRES by Layle Giusto, a light and funny story of a 1990s kind of love. Terry Redding, a mother now divorced and laid off from her job, needs a new place to work. Enter Mark Holden, a businessman and single father who needs a live-in housekeeper. Terry can't help but be amazed at the instant sexual attraction between them; however, her new employer seems determined to keep things strictly platonic until an arrangement of mutual convenience flames into a love neither can resist—or deny. And until Mark makes Terry one final, irresistible offer . . .

Also, look for our latest Valentine offering, a VALENTINE KISS, a collection of stories by authors Carla Fredd, Brenda Jackson, and Felicia Mason. These stories are ideally suited for this special season of hearts and flowers. In all three tales, lovers find each other with a little help from cupid. Romance is like a box of Valentine's day chocolate: Sweet, delectable, and filled with surprises.

The following are previews of HOME FIRES and A VALENTINE KISS. Take a peek . . . and enjoy.

HOME FIRES

by
Layle Giusto

Mark had been watching when Terry came back from the telephone and didn't miss how upset she was. Seeing her in that state angered him. He'd been on the verge of demanding she tell him about the call when he'd forced himself to remember that he had no rights over this woman. He'd never thought of himself as a possessive man, but obviously, when a woman lived in his home, he felt territorial about her. At least he hoped that was all it was.

He wondered if it was a man and had she seen him the other night when she went out.

"Daddy," Yvette touched his shirt, "my science teacher, Mr. Fonda, is getting married."

"Foolish man," Mark said before thinking. "So, do we have homework? As soon as dinner's finished, we'll get with it." He pretended it was a chore, but everyone knew how much he enjoyed doing this with the girls. Certainly they did as they giggled and went for their books.

Since he'd started coming home early, he'd found himself eagerly anticipating this little ritual of assisting the children. To be home meant he had to bring a huge briefcase of work. Also, he had to make many of his calls from the house. Still, so far, the business wasn't suffering because of it. He only wished he could say the same thing about his best friend and partner, James

McNeil. But he didn't want to think of that right now. He wanted to enjoy the moment.

That was another new plus about spending more time at home—the quality of his life. He didn't have more hours in his day and was still as harassed as ever, but he'd gained the ability to live in and even enjoy the moments as they came. He had long periods of being caught up in the joy and fun of the present. It was like a gift. Naturally, Redding picked that moment to intrude upon his pleasure.

"You shouldn't turn Yvette against marriage," Terry said from across the room.

The remark sounded like a reprimand. Mark gazed back and was immediately taken with how charming she looked.

"What are you talking about?"

"Don't you want Yvette to have a happy marriage?"

It took him aback. "Any little twerp coming around to mess with my daughter had better be very careful. I'll break his kneecaps."

"Don't you want her to have children? Don't you ever think that you might some day have grandchildren?"

He was startled. Yvette, a woman? he thought. That seemed impossible. True, he liked to tease her about having to marry a rich man who would buy her some teeth, but that didn't mean he really thought she would ever grow up. "I never thought of that," he admitted. "Maybe when I'm an old man."

"How old would you want to be before she gets married?"

"You know. Like when I'm eighty or something.

Then I'll be too old to beat her suitors up." He smiled impishly.

"Let me see." She paused to look up as she counted. "If you're eighty, that would make Yvette—fifty-something?"

"For Pete's sake! Do you have to take everything literally?" The woman was always telling him how to be a father. What a nuisance she could be.

"I'm only saying that you don't want to turn her against marriage with your—um—ideas."

"What's wrong with my ideas about marriage? I'm perfectly right, and all you have to do is look around you at all the messy lives to see what I mean. And if you turn on the television, the images of marriages will make you want to upchuck . . ."

At that moment, the girls returned and the conversation dropped, but he did look at Yvette thinking that Terry was right. His daughter wouldn't always be his little girl. Someday she would be a woman.

They paired off as had already become their regular way of handling the children's homework. Makeda was a math whiz and she joined him while Yvette instinctively went to Terry, who knew how to be more patient. His old den took on a cozy warmth. His chest felt tight.

He glanced across the room and deliberately avoided the sight of Terry's legs where they were curled under her. Her skirt rode up. Instead, he allowed himself only to look at the relaxed Yvette. His daughter had actually put on a pound or two on Terry's rather suspicious food.

"Mark?" Makeda's little impatient-sounding voice brought his attention back to her efforts.

"I was paying attention all the time," he said, and smiled as he pulled one of her long, thick braids.

But he found himself looking up again, and this time, his gaze went right to Terry's exposed knees. Sure enough, his pants felt as if they were going to burst.

Some time later, Makeda had finished her homework and Mark knew that he hadn't been as much help as usual because he'd been totally distracted with Terry in the room. One time she'd caught him staring at her and he'd thanked God that his complexion was too dark to reveal the blush. She'd only smiled companionably at him and in her innocence had had no idea that she was sharing that cozy moment with a raving sex fiend.

Terry simply looked relaxed and happy. Suddenly, it hit him that she was a beautiful woman, that all she needed was to relax and be happy and she would become the truly beautiful woman that she was obviously meant to be. But she then suddenly looked uncomfortable with the eye contact and glanced away. He only hoped that she wasn't psychic, because he'd hate to have her read him right at that moment.

When everyone was finished, Mark stayed in his chair until he could get up without telegraphing to everyone what had been on his mind. The really worrisome thing was not that he found Terry Redding attractive; any man would go that far. No, the truly scary thing was that he realized that he was buying into this whole package.

He was enjoying the home cooking, though eating one of Terry's meals was quite an adventure, not to mention the less-than-spotless house. He didn't mind picking up a little, as long as he could have the package, the kids, the shared laughter, watching the children as well as admiring Terry's feminine charms. He wanted it all. He'd been dreaming about being a patriarch and having a son.

I must be crazy. Here I am, still daydreaming about the happy family out of the old TV sitcoms. Am I going to get suckered into that crap again? No! The only thing missing is a dog named Fido to bring my slippers and pipe. Well, maybe not the pipe; but the son would sure be nice.

Well, he thought, what's wrong with that? Most men want to settle down at some point in their lives. So, maybe I've finally reached that point at thirty-four. Isn't that why I bought this huge, impractical house? But suddenly, from nowhere, came a really scary thought: for all of that he'd need a wife. How the hell can I have a family without a wife? It was enough to stop those cozy thoughts dead in their tracks.

He glanced at the clock, and realizing that it was still early, he got the idea of calling one of his old girlfriends. Who knew—maybe he could convince one of them to go out for a drink or something. That "something" was really the watchword, he knew. *Well, it's better than sitting here, making mind pictures of Terry, who probably never even had such a thought.*

He walked right past his office, never giving the briefcase a second glance. There was no way he could concentrate with his hormones raging this way. He went into his bedroom, where he picked up his address book and flicked through it. He'd never been good at this dating bit and knew that with the long time that he'd been inactive, he would more likely get turned down. He called an old friend, thinking that she was more aware of the score than most. She never wanted more than he was willing to give.

He was surprised when Nora agreed to have a drink with him and they made plans to meet at one of the local watering holes. Mark was in and out of the shower in minutes, and now something funny occurred. He had been so eager, yet perversely, he now found that he didn't want to leave the house. He felt as if by going outside, he was leaving all the warmth and happiness.

But he needed to get out before he started wanting Fido to bring his slippers again. Even the thought that such an idea could have occurred to him was more than he wanted to admit. Mark hurriedly finished dressing and was rushing out when he stopped to tell Terry where he was going.

The three of them were watching television in the den and once again, he felt drawn to join them. But in the mood he was in, he suspected that he'd better keep moving before he made a move on Terry Redding. When she stopped trying to punch his lights out, she'd probably call the police and truthfully, he wouldn't be able to blame her.

"Eh, Terry, I'm going out for a couple of hours."

He couldn't bring himself to face her. He kept his glance on the girls. He felt that she would know why he was leaving and he wanted her to say something to stop him. But what that could be, he hadn't a clue.

Terry glanced up to find Mark had totally changed his clothes and looked as if he were going to a wedding. From out of the blue, she was really angry. *I sit*

*around here all day, taking care of his child and cook-
ing and cleaning while he goes out as soon as he can.
I can smell the damned aftershave from here. He's all
dressed up to go out tomcatting, as my grandmother
used to say.*

Even to her, that train of thought was insane. So
what if she cooked, cleaned, and babysat? Wasn't that
what he paid her for? she reminded herself. But it did
little to cool her rising temper.

"Okay," Terry said, and surprised herself by how
cool she sounded. Then, to make the act more natural,
she forced herself to look at the television, despite the
reality of not being able to see anything but red. For
some reason, he paused there in the doorway. She
wanted to yell and ask him why he didn't leave already.
It was a miracle, she thought, that she was able to
appear so calm when she was this mad. Am I jealous,
she wondered, and then pushed the thought away.

There was no way she was jealous, she decided. She
knew the heartache of getting emotionally involved
with a man. She had seen her mother turn into a bitter,
dispirited woman when she was so young. She had
heard many times the lessons that her grandmother
taught. And then, despite all that, she had deluded herself and married Ronald. With all those learning experiences, there was no way she was ever going to
forget them. No more men for her. She had withdrawn
from the fray. If Mark Holden wanted to go tomcatting,
let him have a ball.

Finally he left, closing the door quietly behind him.
Terry heard his car start and move off. She could
barely wait for the end of the show to put the girls to
bed. For some weird reason, she felt weepy. *I'm tired,*

she explained to herself. Fortunately, the girls were rather subdued and went to bed without their usual fuss.

"Do you think Daddy will be back?" Yvette said in a soft little voice.

It made Terry's heart constrict. But in a way, it was actually a good sign. At least the child was becoming comfortable with her feelings. "Of course he will, honey. Your daddy's not going to leave you," she said to reassure the child. When Yvette gave a tired smile and closed her eyes, Terry wished it was as easy to reassure herself.

It simply wasn't working, Mark decided, though he had been the one to call. Nora had agreed, he realized, because she was already planning to go out and didn't want to arrive at the pub without a date. Once they were there, all her girlfriends, those with men and those without, gave him the once over. The whole thing seemed too predatory and reminded him that this was the reason it was often easy to get a date with these women on such short notice.

One of Nora's friends, a woman who had seemed especially close to Nora, pushed a piece of paper into his hand. When he opened it, he found her address written there.

The guys were even worse, and it gave him a glimpse of how he must have appeared when he was playing this same scene. Their whole demeanor said they intended to go to bed with someone and didn't seem too particular about which of the women it would be.

Yet what had he expected? It was the question he'd asked himself several times that night. For Nora did invite him home after a few drinks and he'd demurred, saying something about having to get up for work the next morning. I must be nuts, he kept thinking, but he'd refused.

He didn't feel too pleased with himself as he entered his house. He stood there in the foyer listening, but the lights were out and from the silence he knew that everyone had already retired. He peeked in on the girls and chanced a light kiss on Yvette's brow. Both children were breathing deeply with their own little-girl dreams. He regretted having gone out earlier, wondering what he'd missed.

At Terry's door, he'd wanted to go in but knew it was an insane gesture. Was he going to kiss her brow as he had Yvette's? Not likely, he knew. Instead, he listened, wondering if he'd hear her breathing. But this was crazy, he warned himself, and left to enter his own room.

Terry had lain awake for several hours after Mark had left and for some reason, she thought about Ronald. She remembered how full of ideas she'd been when Ronald had proposed. She had wanted to believe that despite all she'd seen to the contrary, she could make a happy marriage with Ronald. He'd been full of promises, too. She'd even helped him finish school. But Ronald had only used her. Still she believed in love and marriage. She considered it a sacred trust but had long ago decided it was not for her.

A few hours later, Terry heard Mark come in. Despite her anger, she had waited for him. She kept imagining how he could go off the road and into a ditch. But such thoughts only made her temper worse. Once again, she was tempted to go out and confront him, only she couldn't think of any reason for why she was so angry. Instead, now that he was home, at least she could stop worrying and turn over and go to sleep.

She heard him when he came and stopped outside her door. She held her breath, wondering why he waited there so long. The temptation to get up and see what he wanted was quickly quashed. Some instinct made her wait too long, and soon he was gone.

She sighed heavily and turned over to sleep. That's when she realized that she wasn't really angry anymore. He's a grown man, she thought, and he has every right to go out whenever he wants.

What's wrong with me, she wondered, just before sleep claimed her.

MADE IN HEAVEN

by
Felicia Mason
from *A Valentine Kiss*
Arabesque's
Valentine's Day collection

Eric Fitzgerald kicked his feet up on the credenza behind his desk and looked out the window and over the courtyard. He smiled. The cupid fountain in the courtyard had been his idea. It was a cold but clear winter day, so no water fell from the fountain and no people gathered on the stone benches strategically placed around the courtyard. But Eric liked what he saw out his window today.

At thirty-five years old, Eric had everything he wanted: good friends, a thriving company, and all the creature comforts a man could desire. He already claimed as his own the house, the cars, even the boat, although he rarely had time to take it out on the water.

For the past twelve years, ever since he opened the first A Match Made in Heaven office, he'd been nonstop focused on his company and the goals he'd set for himself after graduating from college. He'd built the matchmaking agency from a room with a fax machine and an extra telephone line in his apartment to five independent sites across Virginia.

And Netanya had been by his side through most of it. She'd come on board in the second year and brought fresh ideas and a feminine perspective to the agency. Together they'd made a lot of money and put together a lot of happy couples. He and Netanya, as special guests, had attended more weddings than he could remember. And according to the letters and photographs from clients and former clients, there were several little children named either Eric or Netanya, in honor of the people who brought their parents together.

It was Valentine season, one of the busiest and most profitable times of the year for A Match Made in Heaven. Business was booming at all five locations, but particularly in the headquarters site here in Newport News and in Alexandria. Opening the Alexandria office in northern Virginia had been a stroke of genius, Eric thought. With all the metropolitan Washington, D.C., area to pull from, A Match Made in Heaven was so successful there that he and Netanya had been considering moving the headquarters to Alexandria.

But Newport News was home. And life was perfect.

Eric dropped his legs and stood up. Shrugging out of the pinstripe suit jacket, he loosened his tie.

"So why does it feel like something's missing?" he asked his empty office.

Since no answer was forthcoming, Eric glanced at his watch. Netanya was filling in today, doing interviews. Mrs. Randall was back, according to the staff. The spritely old lady had been a client practically since Eric had opened the doors. With Mrs. Randall's track record of either burying or divorcing husbands she found through A Match Made in Heaven, Eric wasn't sure if she should be counted as a success story or a dismal failure on the agency's part. He smiled. At least Mrs. Randall was happy, he surmised.

"Too bad you can't say the same thing for yourself."

Wondering where that thought had come from, Eric sat down again and turned his attention back to the computer monitor and the end-of-week reports filed from his office managers at the sites across the state.

"Hello," Netanya said, coming forward to greet each woman. "I'm so very glad you chose A Match Made in Heaven."

"I'm Shelley Ward and this is Kalinda Michaels," Shelley said.

"Hi, I'm Val Sanders," Val said, stepping forward and shaking Netanya's hand.

"Hello there. You were chatting with Mrs. Randall in the lobby. It's a pleasure to meet you. Is Val short for something?"

Val couldn't hide the slight grimace. But before she could speak up, Shelley cut in.

"Her name is Valentine. And coming here to find a love match is our birthday present to Val. She'll be thirty on Valentine's Day. Frankly, we are all fed up to here," she said, indicating her forehead, "with shallow, egotistical mama's boys. We three are looking for real men, men who know how to treat a lady." The swing of her head sent Shelley's long braids flying.

"Please, call me Val," Val told Netanya.

"Well, happy birthday a few days in advance. I hope we can make this a very special Valentine's Day for you. Why don't you all have a seat and Shelia will tell you a little about A Match Made in Heaven," Netanya said.

The dynamics of this group was interesting, Netanya thought as she studied the three while Shelia gave the introduction to the dating service. If first impressions were important, and Netanya knew they were, Shelley was the dynamo, in-your-face one, and Val, who obviously had a hangup either about her name or about turning thirty, was the conservative one. Netanya hadn't missed the small shudder and the grimace Val tried to conceal at Shelley's introduction of her. Kalinda, who had yet to say anything, was possibly the shy one in the group. But Netanya wanted to know more about Val.

Val listened to Shelia explain about databases and compatibility, about expanding one's horizons and meeting the challenges and expectations of the dating scene. She shook her head. Once Shelley got on a roll, there was no stopping her. This Netanya woman, the pink-and-white cloud, probably thought she was some desperate type, eager to get a man. That wasn't the case at all. Val had plenty of dates. The problem was in the quality of the men.

"We at A Match Made in Heaven cannot guarantee that you'll meet the partner of your dreams," the counselor said, "but we do guarantee that you will be introduced to a significant number of people who meet the qualifications you have, and, more important, people who will expand your social contacts. If, in the process, you meet your match made in heaven, we all win. You will have entered a terrific relationship and maybe, just maybe," she said, smiling, "we'll get to add you and your match to our display of Heavenly Couple Nuptials."

Kalinda laughed at the name. "What does that mean?"

The counselor indicated the back wall in the small room. "Heavenly Couple Nuptials are the weddings of our clients. Many people meet their lifemates through our introductions."

Val glanced at the photographs of smiling couples, then crossed her legs and sat back in her chair. "And how many of your couples actually stay together after these hasty introductions and nuptials?"

Netanya fielded the question. "Well, Val, like any marriage, whether the partners meet through a dating service, a personal ad, through friends, or by accident, each person has to work on the relationship. Relationships don't just happen. Some of our clients are repeat clients. Not everyone who comes through our doors is looking for a life partner. Some people just want to meet new people, to expand their social network."

"You haven't answered my question," Val pointed out. "What's the divorce rate among your clients?"

"I don't have exact figures, but I don't believe the rate is any greater than those who meet without the assistance of a service like this one."

Val didn't look convinced. "All day long I listen to couples who were once so in love, scream at each other, and divvy up their personal property as if each china plate and copper pot were the crown jewels."

"You're a divorce attorney?" Netanya asked.

"No," Shelley piped up. "She's a court reporter who has had the unfortunate assignment of being sent to divorce court. She listens to all this poison every day and then transfers all that negativity to her own relationships. Everybody is not like the couples you meet in court, Val."

"Thank you for that analysis, Dr. Ward," Val said. "If I recall correctly, you have a Ph.D. in political science not in psychoanalysis."

Shelley and Kalinda laughed at Val's tone.

"Don't mind Val," Kalinda said. "She had a bad date last night, plus she gets weird like this around her birthday every year. We're used to it."

"I do not get weird. And some friends you two are."

Netanya decided it was time to separate the women. Sometimes a group of friends meeting together worked. Other times it didn't serve any of the prospective clients very well. This looked like it was shaping up to be one of those times. "What we'll do now is tell each of you how the process works and then you can take a tour of the facility. Shelia, if you would get Marie to work with Kalinda. Val, you can stay here with me. Shelley can go with you, Shelia."

When the room was cleared, Netanya began again with Val.

"Tell me why you're here."

"I'm here under duress, Ms. Gardner. Look, I'll be totally honest with you. This was not my idea. This is Shell and Kalinda's birthday present to me. We went to lunch this afternoon and they sprang this matchmaking thing on me. I'm here to humor them. I'm not looking for a partner, a relationship, or a match made in heaven. As a matter of fact, I decided just last night that being single has its merits."

Val got up and walked to the wall of wedding and couple photographs. "I don't believe in love at first sight. And I definitely don't believe that all these people met here and then lived happily ever after."

Netanya watched the woman named Val. She was tall, full-figured, articulate, and pretty. She was a young black professional woman—a highly sought after commodity with a great deal of the agency's male clients. Without consulting a single computer file, Netanya knew there was a pretty long list of men who would jump at the chance to go out with Val. But Netanya had one man in mind.

"As I said before, not every person is looking for happily-ever-after. Some people just want happily-ever-now."

Val smiled, then walked back to her seat. "Now you're talking my language. Romance is a farce, but having fun, now, that's something that I like."

"What do you like to do?"

Val settled in her chair and crossed her legs. "Do you mean like on a date?"

"Not necessarily. Just in general," Netanya clarified.

"I love to garden. I've converted a section in my condo to something of an indoor garden and hothouse. I like to do volunteer work. I tutor children on Wednesdays and Saturdays in connection with a youth program and recreation center here in Newport News and I love the water."

Netanya grinned. "So do I. I like to just soak up the sun. Are you a sunbathing-on-the-beach type, or are you into water sports?"

"Both. I can't wait for it to warm up enough to get back on the beaches."

"Val, let me tell you how we operate here at A Match Made in Heaven. If you decide that it's something you'd rather not participate in, I'll be happy to redeem your gift certificate."

Val nodded.

"We provide a number of introduction services. You can write what we call a quick sketch letter of introduction that along with your photograph is published in our monthly newsletter. That newsletter is distributed to clients at our five sites across the state."

"Where are your other offices?"

"Richmond, Roanoke, Virginia Beach, and Alexandria," Netanya answered. "Another way we have people from across the state communicate is on-line. If you have a computer with a modem at home, you choose who you'd like to contact or you can come here to the agency and log on. We also have videotape and audiotape introductions. Why don't I show you our studios now? And I'll get a copy of the newsletter for you."

Later that evening as she dressed for a dinner she was attending, Val thought about Netanya Gardner and A Match Made in Heaven. Val, Shelley, and Kalinda had all ended up doing videotape introductions. Kalinda had also opted for the newsletter photograph. An on-site makeup artist had calmed Shelley's fears about shiny skin on the videotape.

Val shook her head. "You know this is crazy," she told her reflection. Then, deciding as long as Conroy Franklin wasn't in the agency's database of bachelors, maybe it might be fun. Netanya Gardner was right. There was no law that said you had to marry the people you were introduced to. Just have some fun. Looking at it that way didn't seem quite so unpalatable. And the Gardner woman got credit: She never made a single comment or joke about Val and Valentine's Day.

Val applied a touch of mascara to her eyelashes, then got her coat and headed to the community center for the reception.

The first person her gaze landed on as she did a quick scan of the room was Netanya Gardner. The matchmaker had traded her pink and white ruffles for a matching pale pink blazer and tank dress. In the dead of winter, the pink should have looked ridiculous. Not on Netanya. She carried it off very well. And the tall, brown-skinned man standing next to her seemed quite appreciative as he gazed down at the petite woman.

Two things immediately struck Val about the man: his thick eyebrows and his hands. She wondered what it would feel like to smooth those eyebrows. And those hands. One was wrapped around the drink glass he casually held. He had strong, big hands, the kind that molded and shaped a woman's body as they stroked and stoked physical fires. With a skill born from years of the subtle once-over, Val took in the rest of him. He had a lean but athletic build. About six feet tall, she guessed, maybe six one.

The banded collar of the white linen shirt he wore buttoned to his neck precluded the necessity of a tie. Val liked the casual, elegant look. As a matter of fact, she had to admit, she liked the whole package. A lot. This brother was together.

Her gaze was drawn again to those hands. She wished she could see his fingers. Over time, Val had come to the belief that the width, length, and form of a man's fingers was in direct proportion to . . .

"Val! How nice to see you here," Netanya said. The cheery woman touched the man's sleeve, and the two advanced the few steps needed to reach Val.

As she watched them approach, Val's gaze slowly traveled up the man's tall form until she met his own laughing eyes. He knew she'd been checking him out! Val flushed, then blushed.

Then she extended a hand to Netanya. "Hi, there. Long time no see," she kidded.

Instead of shaking her hand, Netanya pulled Val to her for a quick hug, as if the women were friends who hadn't seen each other in a while.

Netanya then turned to the man. "Val, I'd like you to meet Eric Fitzgerald. Eric and I are partners at A Match Made in Heaven. Eric, this is Val Sanders. She lives in the city."

Val extended one trembling hand to Eric. What was it about this man that made her so restless? For goodness' sake, she thought, he's not the most handsome man you've ever met. He was okay: nice build, nice hands. Then he smiled at her and Val was lost. That dazzling, perfect, fun-filled smile made her knees weak and her heart race.

"Hello," she got out, pleased that her vocal cords still worked. "How do you do?"

"How do *you* do?" he said, taking her hand.

But it wasn't a greeting, it was a caress. He held her hand far too long, then let his fingers trail over her palm as he released her.

Off in a distance somewhere, Val was aware that Netanya was talking, but she was one hundred percent focused on this man, this Eric Fitzgerald, who with a smile and a handshake had her wondering things that she shouldn't be wondering about a stranger. Like how those fingers would feel in her hair, on her breasts. And what *he* would feel like all over her.

Eric was enchanted. He was also quickly becoming aroused. It had been a while since a woman had given him such a deliciously thorough once-over. If the pretty color in her cheeks was any indication, she was embarrassed at having been caught at it. Eric smiled. The one thing he liked above all else was a substantial woman. This one had curves in all the right places. And she was incredibly beautiful.

Her skin was clear, the color of sweet toffee. Her curly hair was pinned up in the back. Eric wondered how long it fell when it was down. Would her hair be as soft as her skin looked?

The button-pearl earrings at her ears matched the buttons on the suit she wore. Eric let his gaze, as bold as hers had been, wander down the rest of her. The skirt stopped a couple of inches above her knees. Eric took a deep breath. He was a leg man, and this woman got a perfect score in that department. They went on forever. He wondered if she preferred stockings over pantyhose. He definitely had a preference. He smiled at the thought.

"Any friend of Netanya's is a friend of mine," he said.

Val swallowed. "Do you two volunteer here at the center?"

"I do," Netanya answered. "I've been working with the children for about three months now." With a playful elbow in his side, she nudged Eric. "I've been trying to get Eric here to volunteer some of his time. The young ones need positive male role models, particularly the boys."

"Are you a volunteer?" he asked Val.

"Yes," she said, wondering where the slightly breathless tone had come from. Get yourself together, Valentine, she scolded herself. "I work with the kids on Wednesday afternoons and Saturday mornings. I've been coming here for a couple of years."

"Netanya, you've finally convinced me," Eric said. But with eyes only for Val, he added, "I think I'll sign up for Wednesday afternoons and Saturday mornings."

They chatted for a few minutes until Val was called away by an acquaintance.

Since she didn't believe in love at first sight, Val could only conclude that her reaction to Eric Fitzgerald was a major case of lust at first sight. And lust, she knew, was easy enough to deal with: If you ignored it, it eventually went away. The only thing was, Val had a sinking feeling that this wasn't going to go away. Not when from across the room she could feel him watching her. And she responded, at least physically.

Now Val looked up, and sure enough Eric was staring in at her. He smiled when their gazes locked and Val put a hand out to the nearest support.

That support happened to be the back of the center director. The man turned around.

"Oh, Val. Let me introduce you to a couple of our other volunteers. Because you all come in at different times and on different days, you volunteers never get to meet each other."

Val let herself be pulled into the conversation. But her thoughts were across the room with Eric Fitzgerald. She'd only just met him, but she felt connected to him in a way that surprised, and, to some degree, annoyed her. She felt almost as if she'd known him, now and through time. The feeling was disconcerting at best, and at worst . . . Val positioned herself so she could see Eric Fitzgerald. Words just didn't exist. The man was gorgeous.

Watch for these upcoming Arabesque romances:

A VALENTINE KISS with Carla Fredd, Brenda Jackson and Felicia Mason (February 1996)
HOME FIRES by Layle Giusto (February 1996)

CHOICES by Maria Corley (March 1996)
PRIVATE MATTERS by Amberlina Wicker (March 1996)

ONLY HERS by Francis Ray (April 1996)
HEAVEN KNOWS by Adrienne Ellis Reeves (April 1996)

FOR THE VERY BEST IN ROMANCE—
DENISE LITTLE PRESENTS!

AMBER, SING SOFTLY   (0038, $4.99)
by Joan Elliott Pickart

Astonished to find a wounded gun-slinger on her doorstep, Amber Prescott can't decide whether to take him in or put him out of his misery. Since this lonely frontierswoman can't deny her longing to have a man of her own, who nurses him back to health, while savoring the glorious possibilities of the situation. But what Amber doesn't realize is that this strong, handsome man is full of surprises!

A DEEPER MAGIC   (0039, $4.99)
by Jillian Hunter

From the moment wealthy Margaret Rose and struggling physician Ian MacNeill meet, they are swept away in an adventure that takes them from the haunted land of Aberdeen to a primitive, faraway island—and into a world of danger and irresistible desire. Amid the clash of ancient magic and new science Margaret and Ian find themselves falling helplessly in love.

SWEET AMY JANE   (0050, $4.99)
by Anna Eberhardt

Her horoscope warned her she'd be dealing with the wrong sort of man. And private eye Amy Jane Chadwick was used to dealing with the wrong kind of man, due to her profession. But nothing prepared her for the gorgeously handsome Max, a former professional athlete who is being stalked by an obsessive fan. And from the moment they meet, sparks fly and danger follows!

MORE THAN MAGIC   (0049, $4.99)
by Olga Bicos

This classic romance is a thrilling tale of two adventurers who set out for the wilds of the Arizona territory in the year 1878. Seeking treasure, an archaeologist and an astronomer find the greatest prize of all—love.

Available wherever paperbacks are sold, or order direct from the Publisher. Send cover price plus 50¢ per copy for mailing and handling Penguin USA, P.O. Box 999, c/o Dept. 17109, Bergenfield, NJ 07621. Residents of New York and Tennessee must include sales tax. DO NOT SEND CASH.